HAVING IT BOTH WAYS

"Starlight," Ben said succinctly. "What about Starlight?"

"What about him?" Carole asked in a tiny, strangled voice, clutching the saddle rack beside her for support.

Ben shrugged, still watching her carefully. "Have you been thinking much about him? Since, you know, Samson came?"

"Sure," Carole said quickly. But then she stopped herself. "Uh, sort of, I guess. What do you mean?" Ben was so hard to understand sometimes—she didn't want to jump to any conclusions about what he was trying to tell her.

This time he was silent for so long that she was sure he'd decided to drop the whole subject. But finally he spoke again. "You can't have it both ways," he said. "It's not fair. Starlight needs more than that. He deserves it."

Don't miss any of the excitement
at PINE HOLLOW,
where friends come first:

#1 *The Long Ride*
#2 *The Trail Home*
#3 *Reining In*
#4 *Changing Leads*
#5 *Conformation Faults*
#6 *Shying at Trouble*
#7 *Penalty Points*
#8 *Course of Action*

And coming in December 1999:

#9 *Riding to Win*

PINE HOLLOW™

COURSE OF
ACTION

BY BONNIE BRYANT

BANTAM BOOKS
NEW YORK • TORONTO • LONDON • SYDNEY • AUCKLAND

Special thanks to Sir "B" Farms and Laura and Vinny Marino

RL 5.0, ages 12 and up

COURSE OF ACTION

A Bantam Book / October 1999

"Pine Hollow" is a trademark of Bonnie Bryant Hiller.

ISBN 0-553-49286-1

Published simultaneously in the United States and Canada.

Bantam Books are published by Bantam Books, a division of Random House,
Inc. Its trademark, consisting of the words "Bantam Books" and the portrayal
of a rooster, is Registered in U.S. Patent and Trademark Office and in other
countries. Marca Registrada. Bantam Books, 1540 Broadway, New York, New
York 10036.

PRINTED IN THE UNITED STATES OF AMERICA

OPM   0 9 8 7 6 5 4 3 2 1

My special thanks to Catherine Hapka for her help in the writing of this book.

ONE

"Don't let her shy away from the road," Carole Hanson called, tightening her reins as a large delivery truck roared past on the two-lane highway near where she and Stevie Lake were riding. "She needs to be ready for any distractions that may come up when she's in the ring—you can't let her forget you're in charge."

Stevie gave Carole only a brief, disgruntled glance, saving most of her concentration for her horse, a spirited bay mare named Belle who was currently prancing sideways and shaking her head. "It's okay, girl," Stevie murmured, using all her riding skills to stop the mare from skittering away from the loud noise. She could tell the horse had been startled by the truck—the quiet country road was sparsely traveled, especially at four o'clock on a Thursday afternoon, and not a single vehicle had passed them in the five minutes they'd been trotting along the grassy verge.

Once the truck had disappeared around a bend, Belle settled down. Stevie gave her a pat, then turned her away from the road and onto a faint path that led through a line of evergreens and into a broad, sun-dappled field. Even though it was the last day of October, the grass in the field was still green and lush, thanks to the lingering warmth of Indian summer in the girls' northern Virginia town of Willow Creek.

Carole caught up to Stevie on the other side of the trees, matching the pace of the big black gelding she was riding to that of Stevie's horse as she shifted down to a walk. "Sorry if I sounded like Max junior back there," Carole said apologetically, tucking a strand of curly black hair back under her hard hat. "I know you knew what to do."

"No biggie." Stevie grinned at her friend. "I know you can't help it. Anyway, you've got a long way to go before you're as bossy as Max. You didn't say a word about keeping my heels down."

Carole grinned back. "Well, now that you mention it . . ."

Stevie adjusted her position slightly and tossed Carole a sloppy salute. "Thanks for the tip, Max junior," she joked. She knew Carole wouldn't mind the teasing, especially if it involved being compared to Max Regnery, the owner of Pine Hollow Stables, where both girls boarded their horses. Everyone who knew Carole knew that Max was one of her role models, and Stevie knew her better than most. The two girls had been best friends since junior high. Stevie knew that Carole's dream was to work with

2

horses full-time someday soon, just as Max did, although Carole still hadn't decided whether she wanted to be a stable owner and riding instructor or explore some other career involving horses. At sixteen, she still had time to narrow down her choices. But she had gotten a jump start on her goals by taking on a part-time job at Pine Hollow.

Stevie glanced forward between Belle's pricked ears, automatically judging the footing ahead and noting the brief incline at the far end of the field. The sun felt warm on her face, and she was enjoying the nice weather, the fresh air, and the feeling of the responsive horse beneath her.

But this was different from the many pleasure hacks she and Carole had taken over the years. For one thing, their other best friend, Lisa Atwood, wasn't with them. And instead of meandering through a few of the many miles of quiet, remote trails behind the stable, where the silence was broken only by the sounds of birdsong and the soft clopping of the horses' hooves, Carole had mapped out a wide-ranging course that would carry them past as many unusual and distracting sights and sounds as possible. It had begun on a short trail past Max's house, where the stable owner's young daughters and their puppy were playing noisily outside. After a quick jaunt through some thickly wooded parkland, the riders had emerged at a spot where a small stream tumbled down a steep hillside in a splattering waterfall. Taking a short detour past an electrical substation, they had reached the country highway and trotted along it for a short while, passing a cow field and several houses. Now they were leaving the road behind on their way toward a local goat farm.

Despite the unusual route, Stevie was having a wonderful time, as she almost always did when she was riding her horse. It was definitely a pleasant change of pace from all the chores her parents had been making her do at home all week. "This is fun," Stevie commented contentedly, steering Belle around a large stump in the field. She shot Carole a slightly guilty glance. "I mean, I know it's totally serious and everything, too, and that it's supposed to help the horses get used to unexpected sights and sounds or whatever, so they won't get spooked." She shrugged. "But it's nice to just get out and ride like this, Colesford Horse Show or no Colesford Horse Show."

When she said the name of the upcoming event, she felt a little thrill of excitement that belied her casual words. The prestigious Colesford Horse Show was being held in a nearby town in a couple of weeks, and it was attracting top competitors from all along the East Coast. Stevie could hardly believe that she and Belle were really going to be a part of it. The other four riders Max had chosen—Carole, Ben Marlow, George Wheeler, and Denise McCaskill— were the best of the best. Stevie knew she was a good rider, too, but she also knew that it had been a leap of faith for Max to choose her to help represent Pine

Hollow. She wasn't going to let him down if she could help it.

"I know what you mean." Carole glanced over at Stevie and smiled. "Nobody says serious training has to be a drag, right?"

"No way." Stevie grinned and returned her glance. When Carole turned to check on their path, Stevie's gaze lingered on the big black horse her friend was riding. Samson, a talented half-Thoroughbred gelding, had been born at Pine Hollow, but he had only recently returned to the stable after an absence of several years. During that time he had blossomed into an athletic, talented jumper, which was why Max had asked Carole to ride him in the Colesford show. Carole's own horse, an eager bay gelding named Starlight, had always been a good jumper, but Max had thought he wouldn't be a match for the level of competition expected at the show.

Samson should be up to it, though, Stevie thought, still watching the black horse appraisingly. *Carole, too. I know this is going to be a tough show, but if the two of them don't place somewhere in the ribbons in show jumping, I'll eat my hard hat.*

She didn't tell Carole what she was thinking, knowing that her modest friend would only launch into a description of all the stiff competitors she would be facing. Instead she glanced at the farm they were approaching. Just ahead was a small pasture where half a dozen goats grazed, but Stevie's gaze wandered past it to the farmhouse visible just beyond the goats' enclosure. The white frame house was decorated with cutouts of witches and ghosts. A large jack-o'-lantern sat grinning on the slightly sagging front porch, and fake cobwebs drooped from the mailbox.

Stevie's good mood flagged slightly as she took in the decorations. "I can't believe it's Halloween and I'm grounded," she said. "While everyone else is out having fun tonight, I'll be stuck at home, probably helping Mom organize the attic or changing the oil in her car or something. I'm going to miss the whole holiday. If that's not cruel and unusual punishment, I don't know what is."

Carole noticed that Stevie's voice had suddenly taken on a grumpy tone. Halloween had always been one of Stevie's favorite days of the year—it was tailor-made for her fun-loving, adventurous, fearless personality. In her younger days she and her three brothers had found countless ways of getting into all sorts of spooky mischief and causing mayhem, playing endless practical jokes on each other and everyone else they knew. These days they were all a little older and more mature, but Stevie and her twin brother, Alex, still weren't above dressing up and doing their best to scare the trick-or-treaters who came to their door.

"Look on the bright side," Carole advised. "At least your parents are still letting you be in the horse show. That's practically a miracle, right?"

"True," Stevie agreed, tugging firmly at Belle's reins as the mare tried to stretch her neck toward a patch of weeds near the goats' fence. "Plus they're okay with my running Scott's campaign."

"How's that going?" Carole asked. With everything else that had been happening lately, she had almost forgotten that Stevie was in charge of their friend Scott Forester's campaign for student body president at Fenton Hall, the private school that he and Stevie attended. Carole went to Willow Creek High, the local public high school, so she had to rely on Stevie for updates. "Was there any fallout from the party? You know, because, well . . ."

"Nope." Stevie shook her head. "Veronica was as good as her word. She's been telling anyone who'll listen that she and Scott were practically the only ones who kept their heads and didn't drink." She grimaced slightly. "Believe me, it's not easy for me to admit, but Veronica diAngelo has actually been a help. I don't know what we would have done if word had gotten out that Scott was drinking. Even though he really only had a few sips of beer, I'm sure Valerie Watkins's friends would have made him out to be some kind of total boozer loser." She shuddered at the thought.

Carole didn't bother to answer. She still felt shocked when she thought about how many of her friends had started drinking at a party Stevie and Alex had thrown the previous Saturday night. Stevie's older brother, Chad, had left some beer in the garage, and someone had found it. Before long everyone knew it was there, and it had seemed to Carole that almost everyone had been eager to help themselves. It had all come to a screeching halt when a neighbor had called the police, but Carole still remembered how helpless she had felt when she'd realized that the party was spinning wildly out of control.

She urged Samson closer to the fence and let him stretch his head curiously toward the goats that had gathered on the other side, pushing and nipping at each other in their eagerness to get a look at the newcomers.

Stevie nodded at the closest one, a large brown goat with a scraggly beard, one horn, and a surly expression. "What do you think? Doesn't that one there remind you of Veronica?"

Carole giggled as the goat in question bleated loudly. "I think it's insulted," she commented.

"Sorry," Stevie told the goat contritely. "You're right. You're way more intelligent and classy than she is. Better-looking, too." She rolled her eyes. "Plus, you probably don't butt in with your stupid opinions about everything all the time, right?"

At that moment the billy goat turned and butted at another goat that was angling for a position at the fence and let out a loud bleat of annoyance. "I don't know, Stevie," Carole joked. "That sounded an awful lot like something Veronica might say."

"Tell me about it." Stevie snorted. "Ever since

Veronica decided to sink her hooks into Scott, she's been even more obnoxious than usual. She's so busy trying to impress him with how helpful she is to his campaign that she's totally getting in my way."

Carole nodded sympathetically, but she didn't comment. Until a couple of years earlier, Veronica diAngelo had ridden regularly at Pine Hollow, and Carole had learned the hard way that it was usually better to ignore the spoiled, wealthy girl as much as possible. But Stevie had never quite learned that lesson. While age and different interests had softened the two girls' antagonism, Stevie and Veronica could still butt heads like a couple of ornery goats when the right situation arose.

After a moment the two girls rode on, heading for the shortcut through the woods that would lead them back to Pine Hollow. "The worst part," Stevie commented, obviously still thinking about Veronica as she flicked a fly from Belle's dark mane, "is that Scott is actually listening to some of her ideas."

"Really? Like what?"

"Her latest is for Fenton Hall to get in on the Willow Creek High School homecoming dance. Miss Fenton has been promising us a fall dance in a couple of weeks, and since we don't even have a football team and are totally homecoming-deprived, Veronica figured she could convince her to arrange things with your principal to combine the two dances into one big bash."

Carole raised an eyebrow. "Really? But homecoming's this weekend, isn't it?" She scanned her memory, wondering if she'd gotten the date wrong. Sometimes she got mixed up about things that didn't have to do with Pine Hollow, but she definitely recalled hearing an awful lot about homecoming in the morning announcements at school for the past week or so.

Stevie nodded. "The dance is Saturday night. Sounds like an impossible dream, right? But apparently Veronica spent quite a while discussing it with Scott at the party, and they've been working on it all week." She pushed back the cuff of her riding glove and glanced at her watch. "Actually, Scott is meeting with Miss Fenton and Mr. Price even as we speak."

"Hmmm." Carole didn't want to say so, but she had to admit that the idea wasn't as terrible as Stevie was making it out to be. Willow Creek was a small town, and most of the students from the public high school had friends at Fenton Hall and vice versa. While Carole herself wasn't planning to attend the homecoming dance—she had too much work to do at the stable—she was pretty sure most students at both schools would love the idea of holding a joint dance.

Stevie shot her a quick glance as they reached the edge of the woods. "You can say it," she said sourly. "The idea does make some sense. I can admit it. Even if Veronica's the one who thought of it."

"Well, it's probably too late for them to arrange it

for this year, anyway," Carole pointed out diplomatically.

"Don't count on it." Stevie made a face. "Veronica's stupid family connections have brought them this far in less than a week. Who knows what she can pull off in the next two days?"

Carole was a little surprised that Stevie was so down on the dance idea, even if Veronica was the one who might make it happen. *I thought the whole point was to get Scott elected,* she thought. *This sounds like it could only help.*

Suddenly she remembered Stevie's grounding, and a little light blinked on in her mind. *Of course.* Even if Veronica and Scott worked a miracle and the dance came off, Stevie wouldn't be able to enjoy it. She would be sitting home, doing chores to help pay for the damage the party had done to her house, imagining the fun her classmates were having, and wishing she could be right there with them, dancing with her boyfriend, Phil Marsten, and having a good time.

She decided it was time to take Stevie's mind off all that. "Belle looks good today," she said, glancing at Stevie's mare. "You two might just surprise everyone in the dressage competition."

"Thanks." Stevie's expression brightened slightly. "She does look good, doesn't she?" She leaned forward in the saddle and patted her horse affectionately. "I just hope I can keep up with her." She

11

nodded at Carole's mount. "I guess I don't have to tell you how awesome Samson looks."

Carole grinned. "Nope. But it's always nice to hear." She was proud of the training she'd done with the big black horse. Samson had already been in terrific shape when he'd arrived at Pine Hollow, but thanks to Carole's tireless work, he was now in peak condition. "He seems to get better and stronger and smarter every day."

"Thanks to you," Stevie pointed out.

"Thanks to *him*," Carole corrected, ducking slightly to avoid a branch hanging over the trail. "He's the best horse I've ever worked with. I sometimes think he's teaching me just as much about jumping as I'm teaching him. It's like sometimes you find a horse, a special horse, and you feel like you're really speaking the same language, you know?"

Stevie patted Belle again and smiled. "I know."

Carole sighed happily as she thought about the upcoming competition. She couldn't wait to show off what she and Samson could do together. "I've never really felt this way about a show before," she commented. "I mean, I usually have an idea that I could do pretty well, or I know I probably shouldn't be entering. But this time it's like there's nothing we can't do. I'm not even talking about ribbons. It would be nice to win, but this time it's really like Max is always telling us: I just want to go out there and do my very best. For my own sake, and for

Samson's, too. He doesn't deserve anything less, and I don't want to let him down."

"Whoa," Stevie joked. "I knew you were smitten with our friend here, but this is sounding serious. Maybe you should just ditch ol' Starlight altogether and get your dad to buy Samson for you for your birthday."

Carole blinked, startled by her friend's words. For one thing, she'd almost forgotten that her seventeenth birthday was coming up in less than three weeks. But more importantly, the very idea of replacing her own horse with Samson gave her a strange feeling in the pit of her stomach.

It's probably because I've never really thought about the two of them together like that, she told herself. *They're so totally separate. I mean, Starlight is my horse, and I love him as much as ever. How could Stevie even joke about my giving him up?*

Suddenly she noticed that Samson was shaking his head, and she realized she'd tightened up on the reins without meaning to. She loosened them immediately, sending the big gelding a mental apology.

But she still felt a bit tense as she thought about Stevie's careless remark. She'd owned Starlight for so long now that it was something she took for granted. He was a part of her life in the same way that her father was, or her best friends. She couldn't imagine tossing him aside for another horse, any more than she could imagine tossing aside any of the people she cared about.

But where does that leave Samson? she thought. *Isn't he an awfully big part of my life these days, too?*

She knew the answer to that without having to put it into words, even in her own mind. She had loved Samson even before his return to Pine Hollow. And with every day that she worked with him, rode him, and took care of him, her feelings for him grew stronger and stronger. . . .

Just then a starling darted past right in front of the horses' noses, and Samson shied violently. Carole managed to keep her balance despite her distraction and moved with the horse as he nearly careened into a tree. Setting to work with her legs, voice, and reins, Carole did her best to soothe Samson.

When she was back in control and Samson was walking along calmly again, Carole heaved a sigh of relief. "That was close," she told Stevie, who had been carefully keeping Belle back to prevent Samson's sudden panic from infecting her as well.

"Nice work." Stevie urged Belle forward, quickly catching up to Carole again on the wide, smooth trail. "He really trusts you."

Carole nodded, feeling uncomfortable as Stevie's previous comment popped into her mind again. *Don't be ridiculous,* she told herself. *She was just joking about that. Getting all worked up about a silly joke makes about as much sense as—as freaking out because a bird flies by. You're allowed to love Starlight and Samson. No one is forcing you to choose between them.*

"Can we trot?" she asked Stevie, doing her best to

keep her voice normal. She didn't want Stevie to guess what she'd been thinking—she felt stupid enough about it as it was. "I promised Max I'd help out with the Halloween party after the intermediate riding class lets out, and it's getting late."

"Sure." Stevie clucked to Belle, sending her into a brisk trot. "Catch us if you can!"

Carole smiled and urged Samson forward after her.

TWO

"Stop looking at your watch," Alex Lake pleaded, grabbing Lisa Atwood's hand across the Formica tabletop. "It reminds me that I have to go back to prison soon."

"Sorry." Lisa squeezed her boyfriend's hand. "I just don't want you to be late. Your parents might decide not to let you go to soccer, either, and then I'd never see you at all."

Alex sighed and dropped her hand, picking up his spoon and scooping up a bite of ice cream from the dish in the middle of the table. "I know," he muttered. "You're right. It just really sucks, you know?"

"I know." Lisa watched her boyfriend sympathetically, wishing there were something she could do to smooth his furrowed brow and banish the depressed expression in his hazel eyes. But his parents had grounded him for the foreseeable future, and she and Alex were just going to have to deal with it. "Look on the bright side," she told him as cheerfully as she could manage. "At least you *are* still allowed to be on the soccer team, so we can hang out after your games like this, right?"

Alex tugged at the grass-stained jersey he was wearing. "Right," he agreed ruefully. "I guess it pays sometimes to have lawyers for parents." He shrugged and managed a weak grin. "It means we can at least try to plea-bargain."

Lisa was glad to see that his sense of humor hadn't been totally crushed by everything that had happened lately. Until just a week or so earlier, Lisa would have believed that nothing could ever come between her and Alex. Ever since the day some nine months before, when Alex had suddenly gone from being Stevie's cute, slightly goofy twin brother to being the love of Lisa's life, Lisa had been certain that they would be together forever.

But now she realized that things had started to change between them as early as the previous summer. Lisa's parents were divorced, and her father had invited her to spend her summer vacation in California with him and his new family. Alex had never really understood her decision to go, mostly because he was upset at the thought of spending so much time apart.

That was the first thing that came between us, Lisa thought as she watched her boyfriend scoop out another spoonful of ice cream. *And the second thing was Skye.*

Alex had always been jealous of her friendship with Skye Ransom, a handsome actor whom Lisa,

Stevie, and Carole had met years earlier. It had been hard enough for Lisa to tell her boyfriend that she had landed a summer job working behind the scenes on Skye's new TV series. How could she tell him about what Skye had said to her a few days before she'd returned home? How could she admit that Alex's worst fears were true—that Skye wished that he and Lisa could be more than friends?

Carole had saved her the trouble, accidentally spilling the secret at the party on Saturday night. Alex hadn't bothered to listen when Lisa had tried to explain that she didn't return Skye's interest—that she loved only Alex. They'd had a terrible fight and broken up, and even though they'd patched up their relationship by the end of the party, things still weren't the same between them. Lisa knew they had a lot of work to do if they ever wanted to go back to normal.

That was why they were sitting at a private corner booth at TD's, the ice cream parlor in the sleepy little shopping center on the edge of town, while Alex's soccer teammates were celebrating their victory at a pizza place across the street from Fenton Hall. Lisa and Alex were trying to spend as much time as possible alone together these days, though it wasn't easy. There was no time for leisurely trail rides at Pine Hollow or for long, romantic dinners on Saturday night—or for much of anything else, for that matter. The only exception Mr. and Mrs. Lake had been willing to make was for soccer practice, though Lisa suspected they might not even have allowed that if they hadn't already promised Stevie that she could continue practicing for the Colesford Horse Show.

"I wish you could have plea-bargained your way to homecoming this weekend," Lisa commented, thinking wistfully of the romantic evening she had expected to share with him at her school's big dance.

Alex snorted. "Fat chance," he muttered. He glanced at her. "I'm sorry, Lisa. I know you were looking forward to the dance." He rubbed the back of his neck wearily. "I was, too. And I was looking forward to that Halloween party we were supposed to go to tonight, and to that new movie we'd talked about catching tomorrow night, and to just getting together with you whenever we felt like it instead of rushing around like this . . ."

"I know." Lisa picked up her napkin and reached across the table to gently wipe a spot of chocolate syrup off his chin. "It doesn't matter. There will be other dances and parties and movies. We'll make it through this."

Alex nodded glumly and stirred his rapidly melting sundae. "I guess."

Lisa sneaked another quick glance at her watch. They didn't have much time left before Alex would have to head home. But she knew she couldn't let him go until she'd brought up the topic that had been gnawing at her since the party. She couldn't put it off one more day. Her stomach clenched when she imagined how he would react to what she needed to tell him, but she couldn't let her nervousness stop her. She had learned her lesson from the Skye fiasco—she wasn't going to put off the hard news too long this time. That could only make things worse.

She took a deep breath, steeling her nerves as best she could. "Alex," she began. "Um, there's something I need to tell you."

He looked up from his dish quickly, clearly recognizing the serious tone in her voice. "What is it?" he asked, looking a bit apprehensive.

Lisa cleared her throat. "It's about Thanksgiving."

"Oh." Alex looked relieved. "Is that all? Listen, don't worry about that. Mom and Dad said you and your mother can still come over for dinner, even though Stevie and I are grounded. In fact, Mom said something just this morning about calling your mom and, you know, officially inviting her."

Lisa gulped, realizing that once again she'd waited almost too long. "That's not it," she said, feeling her throat tighten with anxiety. "It's just—well, I was pretty mad at you. You know. On Saturday night. I—I wasn't sure if we would ever—well, you know. If we were going to . . ." She cleared her throat again, searching for the right words. "Um, the point is, I didn't think our Thanksgiving plans were going to happen after all. So I kind of—well—I called Dad."

Alex's expression darkened slightly; he took on a wary, suspicious look. "Yes?"

"He wanted me to come to California for Thanksgiving," Lisa explained. "I called him from your house after our fight and told him I was coming. I tried to back out the next day," she added hurriedly. "I mean, by then we'd made up, and I had already promised you before the party that I'd come to your house . . ." She shrugged helplessly, avoiding his eyes. "But Dad had already bought my airline tickets over the Internet. Nonrefundable."

Alex didn't speak for a long moment. His expression shifted from shock to sadness to anger. But when he finally answered her, his voice was calm. "That's, um, too bad," he said carefully.

Lisa saw that he was gripping the edge of the table so hard that his knuckles were white. She could tell he was fighting against his own feelings, trying not to freak out at her news, and she appreciated the effort. "I'm really sorry," she said. "I wish I hadn't been so impulsive about it. It's really not like me to just change my mind on the spur of the moment, you know that. But I was so angry and upset . . ."

"I know." Alex forced a small smile. "Um, have you told your mother yet?"

Lisa nodded. "She took it surprisingly well," she said ruefully. "I mean, I'm sure she still hates the fact that I'm going to be with Dad on what's supposed to be a big family-togetherness-type holiday. But I guess she realized that this means she and Rafe will

21

have a whole week to be together without worrying about me walking in on them." She shuddered at the thought of her mother's new boyfriend, a coworker some twenty years her junior. But she quickly pushed the thought aside. Her main concern just then was her own relationship with Alex, not her mother's romance—if you could call it that—with Rafe. "So, uh, what do you think?"

"I wish you weren't going," Alex said frankly. He ran one hand through his short-cropped brown hair and sighed. "But I guess what's done is done, right?"

"I guess so." Lisa opened her mouth to tell him what she knew he wanted to hear: that she wished she weren't going, either. But then she stopped herself. She didn't want to lie to him. She had to trust their relationship to be strong enough to handle the truth, no matter how messy or confusing it was. "I'll miss you, you know that. But I think it might be good for me to go out there for a little while. I miss Dad and Lily a lot." She smiled slightly as she thought about her baby half sister, who had just begun crawling when she'd left at the end of the summer. "And it will give me some time to think about things."

Alex bit his lip. "Like about whether you still want to be with me?" he asked quietly.

"Of course not!" Lisa reached over and grabbed both his hands in her own. "I already know the answer to that. I love you, remember? No matter what happened, or what happens from now on."

"I love you, too." Alex squeezed her hands, but his eyes still looked anxious. "I just wish you could stay here with me, instead of running off to California all the time."

Lisa did her best not to feel annoyed at the comment. *Try to see his point of view. He's just feeling insecure, that's all,* she told herself. *He wants to spend as much time with me as possible. That's a good thing, right? Besides, he's probably not thinking about how much I miss my family out there. He's probably just thinking about Skye . . .*

She couldn't help resenting that, just a little. After all that had happened, hadn't she managed to convince Alex yet that he was the only one she loved? What more did she have to do to prove it to him?

"Anyway," she said, "I hope you can understand how I feel. It isn't easy for me having my family split in two like this."

"I know." Alex gazed at her somberly. "It isn't easy for me, either. I want to be with you all the time, but it feels as though something is always trying to keep us apart. Or some*one.*"

Lisa sighed, saved from responding because the waitress came over to deposit the check for their ice cream. Lisa was glad that she and Alex were talking again. But was having an honest, open relationship supposed to be so hard?

At that moment, Callie Forester was sitting in her living room, frowning over her chemistry notebook

23

and trying to figure out why she couldn't seem to come up with the right answer to the problem she was working on, no matter how many times she went through it. As she erased yet another set of incorrect calculations, she heard the front door swing open and glanced up automatically.

"Hey, Callie," her brother, Scott, greeted her cheerfully, bounding into the room without bothering to remove his windbreaker. "Guess what?"

"Hmmm, let me think," Callie said, more sarcastically than she'd meant to, still irritated by her own inability to comprehend chemistry. "Did your little meeting with the principals go well?"

Scott ignored her sharp tone. "It sure did," he said, rubbing his hands together. His blue eyes were bright with excitement and his broad, handsome face was slightly flushed. "Mr. Price—he's the principal over at Willow Creek High—absolutely loved the idea of putting the schools together. Miss Fenton was a little more cautious at first—you know, because of the timing—but as soon as we managed to convince her we could really make it happen, she jumped on board. She'll be making an announcement tomorrow morning inviting everyone at Fenton who wants to go to the dance to buy their tickets immediately."

Callie couldn't help smiling at her older brother's enthusiasm. She knew there was nothing Scott loved more than a successful campaign—it was a trait he had inherited from their father, a congressman. "Congrats," she told him.

"I know it's pretty short notice, but I think we'll still get a good turnout." Scott shrugged off his jacket and tossed it over a chair, then perched on the end of the couch where Callie was sitting. "Veronica and her friends have been talking up the possibility of the dance all week, so I doubt anyone will be totally surprised."

"It doesn't leave people much time to go dress shopping, though," Callie pointed out.

Scott grinned. "I thought of that, too," he said. "But Ronnie has been asked to the Willow Creek homecoming dance every year since she was in eighth grade. She says it's always pretty informal— not like at our old school, where people treated it almost like the prom."

"That's good." Callie felt a pang as she remembered the prom she'd attended the previous spring in their old hometown on the West Coast, just a couple of months before the family had moved to Willow Creek to be closer to Congressman Forester's office in nearby Washington, D.C. One of the coolest seniors in school had asked her, even though she'd only been a sophomore at the time—being the daughter of an influential politician could do that— and she'd had a fantastic time, dressing to the nines, dancing until her feet hurt, then going to a party on the beach after the dance and staying out until dawn. . . .

But she pushed aside the memory. Scott's mention of Veronica had reminded her of something that had been bothering her for the past few days. "Listen, Scott," she said. "I don't want to be a downer on your big triumphant day or whatever. But I was just wondering if you'd noticed that Veronica is totally into you. She wants you in a big way, and she doesn't care who knows it."

Scott laughed self-consciously. "I don't know if I'd go that far. . . ."

Callie snorted. She had never lacked for male attention—her good looks, as well as her last name, had ensured that—but Scott had always had an almost preternatural ability to make girls swoon wherever he went. He had broken more than a few hearts back in their old hometown, mostly through sheer ignorance of his own charisma.

"Look," she said bluntly. "Don't get me wrong. I'm not especially worried about Veronica's feelings—she strikes me as the type who can take care of herself, you know? And I know you've been so wrapped up in this campaign that you probably haven't stopped to think about any of this. But you should be careful. If you aren't interested in her and you end up blowing her off after the election, well, some people might think you're only using her for her connections." She paused to let her words sink in, knowing there weren't many things more important to Scott than his reputation. "That's not going to make you any friends, no matter how people feel about Veronica herself."

Scott frowned. "Hmmm," he said. "I guess I hadn't thought about it like that. I mean, I sort of like Ronnie. She's sorta cool. But I'm really not looking for anything serious right now. . . ."

"That's what I thought," Callie said, secretly relieved that he didn't return Veronica's feelings. She hadn't relished even the slight possibility of having to spend time with the other girl if Scott started dating her seriously. "So maybe you'd better let her in on the secret soon, okay?"

"I don't know about that." Scott looked reluctant. "I mean, it's not like we've actually been out or anything."

Callie rolled her eyes, amazed as always at her brother's ability to sidestep thorny situations. "Get real," she told him sharply. "As far as most people are concerned, you two are already a couple. If you don't want them to think you're using her, you'd better either sit her down for a little talk right away or just bite the bullet and ask her to the dance."

"Well . . . ," Scott said slowly, rubbing his chin thoughtfully. "Maybe you're—"

The phone cut him off, ringing shrilly from its position on an end table. Callie leaned over to answer it. "Hello, Forester residence," she said automatically.

"Callie?" a tentative male voice replied from the

other end of the line. "Um, hi. It's George. George Wheeler."

Callie gulped. "Oh, hi, George," she replied as her brother winked and headed out of the room. "How's it going?"

"Fine," George said. "Um, so, Callie, about this weekend. Can you—I mean, have you made up your mind yet about Saturday? I don't want to bother you, but, well . . ."

Callie winced, realizing she'd put off this conversation far too long. George had a serious crush on her, and the past Saturday night he had made that quite obvious. He'd followed her around the party at the Lakes' house all night, and she had finally ended up dancing with him and then spending almost an hour talking to him—mostly about horses, since they were both serious competitive riders, George in three-day eventing and Callie in endurance riding. When they had finally parted ways, he'd asked her out for the next Saturday. She had put him off without giving him an answer, telling him she had to think about it.

What am I supposed to do about this? she wondered, feeling uncharacteristically helpless. She pictured George walking down the hall at school—his wispy blond hair sticking up at odd angles, his round face pink and earnest, his clothes always seeming not to hang quite right on his short, pudgy body . . . Then she imagined him the way she'd seen him the last time they'd been at Pine Hollow together. When he climbed into a saddle, George seemed to transform into a different person entirely. He was one of the most talented riders Callie had ever met, which was probably why he was asked to be one of the five riders representing the stable at the Colesford Horse Show in a couple of weeks.

It was hard to reconcile the image of George the spectacular rider with George the sweet but dorky guy. *But why should either of those images make the slightest bit of difference to how I feel about him?* Callie wondered, a bit annoyed with herself. *Since when do I care so much about images?*

She gripped the phone tighter, thinking back to the party, when she had found George's attention irritating and sweet by turns. True, he was the polar opposite of the kind of guys she usually liked. And yes, he had followed her around the party like a pathetic puppy dog. But once she'd started dancing with him, she hadn't been able to ignore how considerate he was. Thanks to a serious automobile accident over the summer, Callie had spent the past few months learning to walk again, and she still relied on crutches to get around. But dancing with George, she'd almost been able to forget that—he had carefully supported her as they'd danced so that her weakened right leg hardly slowed her down at all.

Realizing that she'd been silent for several long seconds, she cleared her throat, still not certain what to say. "Um, Saturday . . . ," she said. "Actually, Scott just came in and told me some news about

Saturday night—we're invited to the Willow Creek homecoming dance."

"What?" George sounded confused. "You and Scott are going to the homecoming dance?"

Callie quickly guessed that George hadn't heard about Veronica's weeklong homecoming campaign. That figured. He was the kind of peripheral guy whom Veronica and her clique ignored as instinctively as they breathed. "Not just me and Scott," she explained patiently. "All of us. Fenton Hall in general." She quickly filled him in on the details.

"Oh," George said when she finished. "Um, well, we could go to that together if you want. Unless you already have other plans, I mean," he added quickly.

Callie bit her lip, still trying to decide what to do. At that moment, out of the corner of her eye, she saw Scott strolling past on his way to the stairs.

I can tell my brother what to do about his love life, but I can't figure out how to deal with my own, she thought. *Still, maybe this dance is a perfect opportunity for me to decide whether I could ever have any romantic interest in George. We won't have to be alone much, we both like dancing . . . and if sparks are ever going to fly, it's bound to happen at a romantic event like that, right?*

She nodded, feeling satisfied with her own logic. "I don't have any other plans," she told George. "I'd love to go to the dance with you."

"Really?" George's voice was so eager that Callie

winced. "That's great! Just great! Um, I mean, thanks, Callie. I'm sure we'll have fun."

"Me too," Callie lied, already wondering if she'd made a huge mistake. "We'll talk about it tomorrow at school, okay?"

She hung up, feeling apprehensive. George had sounded thrilled at the idea of going to the dance with her—so thrilled that it made her perversely certain that there could never be a future for the two of them.

What's my problem? she wondered fiercely. *It's a good thing when a guy likes you, remember? I just need to chill and see what happens. And if I decide things aren't going to work out for us . . . well, I'll just have to deal with that when the time comes.*

THREE

"Juliet!" Carole shouted. "No running in the stable, remember? Max will have a fit if he catches you."

Juliet Phillips didn't seem to hear her. She shrieked loudly and raced out of the indoor ring and down the aisle as a new seventh-grade rider named Brian Chalmers chased her with a handful of whipped cream he'd scooped up from somewhere. Carole sighed and rubbed her head, wondering if she had ever been as giddy and silly as the intermediate riders were acting that day.

"Relax, Carole," Denise McCaskill said kindly as she joined Carole near the punch bowl, depositing a plate full of cookies on the long refreshment table Max had set up for the intermediate riding class's Halloween party. "It's a party, remember? You're going to give yourself an ulcer."

Carole smiled gratefully at Denise, Pine Hollow's petite, friendly, twenty-something daytime stable manager. "I know. I'm just afraid they're going to get too rowdy and scare the horses. Especially Prancer."

Denise brushed back her dark brown bangs, then absently patted the thick braid at the nape of her neck as she turned to survey the scene. Carole followed her gaze, noting that Sarah Anne Porter had borrowed several shiny metal stirrups from the tack room to use as bracelets for her genie outfit and that Alexandra Foster and Justine Harrington were enthusiastically chasing one of the stable cats that had made the unfortunate decision to come around begging for treats.

"Okay, I'll admit they're a little rowdy right now," Denise said calmly, raising her voice as Rachel Hart let out a shriek of laughter from nearby. "But I'm sure they'll settle down when Max gets back from putting the girls to bed." She smiled at Carole, making the tanned skin around her dark eyes crinkle slightly. "They may be kind of giddy, but not so much that they'll forget they're scared of making him mad."

Carole smiled weakly in agreement, but then she sighed. "Still, these parties always seemed to go a lot more smoothly when Mrs. Reg was here," she said, thinking of Max's widowed mother, a kind, calm, capable woman who had helped manage the stable before retiring to Florida a couple of months earlier. "I miss her."

"Me too," Denise agreed. Before she could say anything more, her longtime boyfriend, Red

O'Malley, Pine Hollow's head stable hand, waved frantically at her from across the ring, where May Grover had just tripped and fallen into the apple-dunking tub. "Uh-oh," Denise said. "Looks like Red could use some help. I'd better get over there."

"Okay." Watching her go, Carole decided to take the opportunity to slip away and check on Prancer. Despite Denise's assurances, Carole was concerned that all the noise might be frightening the pregnant mare. Prancer was carrying twins, which automatically made her pregnancy a high-risk one. Just the week before, Max had been worried that she might have lost one of the foals when he couldn't find its heartbeat. In the end the vet had pronounced the mare and both her foals alive and healthy, but Carole knew that could change at any moment, which was why she and Denise and Red and Ben and Max had all been keeping a close watch on Prancer in between their other chores.

She dodged around Alexandra and Justine and made her way out of the indoor ring a few steps behind the terrified stable cat. Ignoring the younger girls as they called for her to stop the cat, Carole rounded the corner into the aisle where Prancer was housed.

A few minutes later, when she was satisfied that Prancer was resting comfortably in her stall, seemingly unfazed by the commotion just down the hall, Carole headed reluctantly back toward the party, taking the long way around the U-shaped stable to make sure none of the other horses were upset by the noise.

"Hey, Topside. How's it going, Windsor?" she murmured, patting the curious heads that poked out of the stalls as she passed. "Don't worry, Barq. The party will be over soon. I hope."

She paused as she reached the next stall, where a very familiar bay face with a lopsided star was watching her approach.

"Hi, boy," she greeted Starlight softly. A weird twinge of discomfort nudged at her as if she'd had a disturbing dream about him that she couldn't quite remember. But it wasn't a nightmare that was pulling at her, she realized a half second later. It was Stevie's comment earlier that day, the one about getting rid of Starlight. . . .

Before she could think about that, a loud, piercing shriek erupted from just down the aisle. Startled, Carole dropped her hand from her horse's neck and turned to see what was going on. She saw that Alexandra and Justine had a different stable cat cornered a few yards down the hall, and they were trying to catch the poor animal. The cat, a big calico, had just jumped onto the narrow top edge of one of the stalls' half doors. Several of the horses stabled nearby had obviously been frightened by the sudden noise—Carole could hear at least one set of hooves connecting with the stable wall, and even Starlight had let out a surprised snort and rolled his eyes.

Her heart in her throat, Carole hurried toward the

35

two younger girls, ignoring Belle, who nickered for her attention as she hurried past her stall. "Hey!" she said urgently, not wanting to shout and scare the horses even more. She grabbed Justine's arm tightly and glared at Alexandra. "What's the matter with you two?"

Justine's face took on the annoyed, stubborn expression Carole had grown to know and dread, but Alexandra looked sheepish. "Sorry, Carole," she whined. "We just wanted to play with the kitties, but they're too shy."

"They're not shy," Carole snapped, exasperated. "They just don't like being grabbed and shrieked at. Can you blame them?" She glanced over and saw that the calico cat had made an escape, her white-tipped tail just disappearing up the wooden ladder to the hayloft. When she looked back at the two girls, Carole spotted someone hurrying toward them from the other end of the hall. She gulped, recognizing Ben Marlow's dark hair and broad shoulders—and his thunderous glare.

"What's going on?" he demanded when he reached them.

Now even Justine looked contrite and slightly nervous. Ben Marlow rarely showed much emotion, at least not when he was dealing with people rather than horses, whose company he clearly preferred. But he was angry now. If there was anyone who could scare the two young offenders more than Max, it was Ben. Carole knew that most of the intermediate riders whispered about the brooding young stable hand behind his back, and she'd once heard Sarah Anne Porter speculate that he would make a perfect crazy ax murderer in a horror movie—good-looking but mysterious and a little scary.

"Nothing," Justine muttered sullenly, peeking up at Ben quickly, then staring down at her feet. "No problem."

Ben looked at Carole questioningly. She shrugged, giving the younger girls a stern glance. "I think it's all under control," she told Ben. "These two were just heading back to the party. Right?"

"Uh-huh," Alexandra squeaked, scurrying down the hall without risking so much as a glance at Ben. Justine followed without a word.

Carole heaved a sigh, glad that the incident was over and even more relieved that it hadn't taken place anywhere near Prancer's stall—especially since the mare was terrified of cats. A quick check was enough to tell her that the horses nearby had already lost interest and settled down in their stalls.

She turned her attention back to Ben, who was staring after the intermediate riders, still looking angry. "Twerps," he muttered. "Shouldn't be allowed in a stable."

Carole shrugged. While she agreed that Justine and Alexandra's behavior had been irresponsible, her annoyance with them was already fading now that it was over and all the horses were safe. She couldn't quite agree that banning them from Pine Hollow was much of a solution. They were young, and they had simply gotten excited and forgotten where they were. It happened. She could remember more than one occasion when she and her friends—especially Stevie, who had been just as irrepressible and exuberant as any of these intermediate riders—had lost their heads and broken one of Max's many stable rules.

"Whatever," she told Ben neutrally, not wanting to start a debate about the younger girls' behavior. Especially not now, when she felt herself blushing, as she still seemed to do whenever she set eyes on him.

Ben hardly seemed to hear her. His thick brows were set in a deep scowl, and his dark eyes were still flashing with anger. "Twerps," he muttered grimly as he turned and peered into the nearest stall. "Better see if everyone's okay."

Carole bit her lip and did as he suggested, glancing into the stall across the aisle. A horse named Congo stared placidly back at her, chewing steadily on a mouthful of hay. *I guess I shouldn't be surprised that Ben is crankier than usual today,* she thought as she moved on to the next stall. *A bunch of hyper Pony Clubbers isn't exactly his cup of tea.* She patted Comanche, who had come to the front of the stall to greet her. *Still, it would be nice if he weren't always so difficult . . .*

She winced as she thought back to the party the previous weekend. She still didn't know why Ben had decided to come. A crowded high-school party wasn't any more his scene than a Pony Club bash. But one thing was certain in Carole's mind—he *hadn't* come because he was interested in getting to know her better. He'd made that abundantly clear.

What was I thinking, asking him to dance like that? she wondered, feeling a hot blush creeping over her cheeks even at the memory. *It's crazy. Ben and I are hardly even friends, let alone . . . Anyway, I can't believe I was such an idiot. It's not like I ever even thought of him that way. Why would I?*

Risking a glance at Ben, she saw that he was looking straight back at her. His frown had faded and he looked thoughtful. As soon as he saw her looking, he jumped and turned quickly back to the horse beside him. "Things look okay," he said gruffly over his shoulder.

"Uh-huh." Carole swallowed hard, hoping he hadn't noticed her hot cheeks in the relatively dim light of the stable aisle. Every time she looked at him now, she remembered how he'd turned her down when she'd asked him to dance, then stood and abruptly left the party. But he hadn't mentioned the incident since, and she certainly wasn't about to bring it up. If he could ignore what had happened, so could she.

I just wish . . . The thought trailed off, and Carole wasn't even sure what she'd been about to wish for. Maybe just that Ben hadn't had such an easy time ignoring what she'd said at the party. *I guess it would be kind of nice if he ever noticed I was alive except when he's annoyed with me,* she thought. *It would be nice to have someone to talk to—a real friend who could understand what I'm all about . . .*

Carole was surprised at her thoughts. She automatically stepped over to the next stall, but she hardly saw the horse dozing in the far corner as she leaned on the half door. Behind her, she heard Ben murmuring softly to the horse he was checking, though she couldn't quite make out his words. He seemed to have his own language that he used only with horses, one much more fluent than his English, which he often seemed to struggle with as if it were a foreign tongue that he'd never quite mastered.

It's not as if Ben exactly invites the idea of his being some kind of—of confidant, she told herself. *It's not even like he's much of a friend most of the time.* She chewed her lower lip thoughtfully. *Anyway, what do I need a new friend for? My own friends are wonderful. I'm lucky to have them.*

She smiled as she thought about Stevie and Lisa. How many years had they been friends now? How many scrapes and adventures and problems had they worked through together? Carole couldn't even begin to count. All she knew was that they would always be best friends, no matter what happened. If she needed further proof of that, all she had to do was remember the way Lisa had forgiven her for accidentally telling Alex about what Skye had said.

Still, it sometimes seems like they're both so busy with other things these days, she thought wistfully. *They both have their boyfriends. Lisa has been working like crazy on her college applications since summer. Stevie is all wrapped up in that school election, and she's really getting involved in the student government at Fenton Hall. . . . Sometimes I'm not sure they even remember how much we all used to love spending all our spare time here.* She glanced around the stable, breathing in the familiar scents, listening to the comforting sounds. *I'm not sure they really understand how important this all still is to me.*

Carole knew that her friends were aware of her dedication to horses. They knew she planned to spend her life working with horses—she had been planning that for as long as she'd known them. When they'd all been younger, the three of them had spent much of their time together discussing horses and riding. But these days, Stevie and Lisa had other interests, other concerns, and Carole occasionally suspected that they didn't quite get her continuing preoccupation with her favorite topic.

Ben's the only other person near my age who never wants to talk about anything else, Carole realized, sneaking another peek at the stable hand. He was holding Belle's head in both hands, his face close to hers as he spoke softly to her. Carole couldn't help smiling slightly at the sight. *Or maybe I should say he's the only other person who never wants to talk* to *anything else.*

At the thought, a giggle escaped before she could

stop it. Ben turned toward her, his expression caught somewhere between curiosity and suspicion.

Carole quickly arranged her face into a bland expression, not wanting him to think she'd been laughing at him. "Everyone over here seems fine," she said matter-of-factly. "I don't think those two big-mouths scared anyone too badly."

"Good." Ben nodded curtly.

Carole bit back a sigh, realizing how crazy her previous thoughts had been. How could she even imagine Ben as a confidant, a true friend? Yes, he was just as wrapped up in horses as she was—but that was just the problem. He wasn't interested in anything except horses, and that included other people.

"Carole."

She had been so involved in her thoughts that she almost didn't hear him. Suddenly realizing that Ben had spoken her name, she looked up quickly. "Huh?" she said. "Uh, I mean, what?"

Ben took a step toward her and then stopped. "I, ah, wanted to say something," he said gruffly, shoving his hands deep into the pockets of his jeans. "About, well . . ."

"Yes?"

He glanced from side to side, looking almost as trapped as that unlucky cat had been a few minutes earlier. But just when Carole thought he was going to mutter an excuse and hurry away, he cleared his throat and spoke again. "I've been wanting to say something."

His voice was so low that she automatically stepped toward him until they were standing face-to-face in the middle of the wide stable aisle. Carole felt her heart pounding, though she wasn't exactly sure why. For some reason, she was suddenly certain that he didn't want to discuss Prancer's special grain ration or whose turn it was to hose down the manure pit. She waited for him to go on.

"About Colesford." Ben tossed his head to get his thick dark hair out of his eyes. For the first time, he met her gaze directly. "About you and—and Samson."

"What about us?" Carole asked, sensing that he had something important on his mind.

"I've noticed you." Ben blinked and coughed, looking uncomfortable. "Uh, I mean, I've noticed how much you—"

"There you are!" a frazzled voice interrupted. Max had just rounded the corner into the aisle where they were standing. He hurried toward them. "So this is where you two are hiding out. Traitors."

Ben took two quick steps back from Carole and turned to face his boss. "Sorry, Max. I was—"

"We were just on our way back—" Carole began at the same time. Laughing awkwardly, she glanced at Ben and then shot Max a contrite smile. "Sorry. We were just checking on the horses."

"Uh-huh." Max looked bemused. "Well, you'd better get back in there before those little heathens decide to toss a couple of saddles on Red and Denise and turn them into bucking broncos."

Carole giggled at the image, though she couldn't help wondering what Max was thinking. Something in his expression made her worry that he was jumping to some wrong conclusions about her and Ben. "We're going, we're going," she hastened to assure him, doing her best to sound as cheerful and normal as possible.

Shooting a quick glance at Ben as they followed Max down the aisle toward the indoor ring, she wondered what he'd been about to say. But whatever it was, it would have to wait. She could already hear the shouts and laughter from just ahead.

Lisa still felt oddly unsettled as she walked the half block from the Lakes' house to her own. She and Alex hadn't talked much on their way home, and even though he'd kissed her good-bye as tenderly as ever, their conversation back at TD's had left her distracted and slightly upset. She wasn't sure what to think about what they'd said to each other, though she was glad that she'd finally managed to tell him about Thanksgiving. That was important.

Noticing that her mother's car wasn't in the driveway, she paused at the mailbox by the curb. She pulled out a thick stack of mail and headed for the door, flipping through the catalogs and advertisements and absently wondering if her mother got any joy out of being on absolutely every mailing list in the world.

She paused on the walkway when she spotted a creamy white, business-sized envelope with her own name on it. Pulling it out of the stack, she clenched it in her teeth and stuck the rest of the pile under one arm. Then she grabbed the long white envelope and checked the return address.

"NVU," she murmured under her breath, her eyes widening. "That was fast." She had sent in her application to Northern Virginia University a little over a month before, knowing that as a state resident she would receive priority treatment. In fact, the school had an early-action program, which meant that they would notify her as soon as they made a decision about her application, but she wouldn't have to respond until May, once she'd heard from all the other schools she'd applied to and made up her mind where she wanted to go.

She slit the envelope with her fingernail and pulled out a small packet of papers. Flipping it open, she saw that the top sheet was a letter with the school's crest emblazoned across the top.

Dear Ms. Atwood, it began. *I am very pleased to inform you that you have been accepted into the Northern Virginia University class of . . .*

She scanned the rest of the letter quickly, feeling a mild glow of pleasure sweep over her. This was an unexpected bright spot in her confusing and difficult day. Even though she hadn't even finished all her applications yet, it was nice to know that she'd already been accepted somewhere. It would make waiting for the other responses a little easier.

Quickly looking through the rest of the packet, she saw another letter, this time from the office of the director of the honors program. *Due to your outstanding academic record,* it read, *you are hereby invited to enroll in the University Honors Program. You have also been awarded a merit scholarship in the amount of three thousand dollars per annum.*

Lisa's eyes widened at the amount. She had almost forgotten the scholarship application she'd sent in along with her other materials—her guidance counselor at school had advised her not to count on receiving any money from the school, since there were only a handful of merit scholarships available.

What do you know? she thought, stuffing the papers back into the envelope and shoving it into her jacket pocket. A chilly breeze lifted her shoulder-length blond hair, making her shiver, and she wrapped her arms around herself and hurried toward the house. *That money will definitely come in handy if I decide to go there.*

But her mind was already shifting back to her earlier thoughts about Alex. She would have plenty of time to figure out what to do about college once all her applications were in. It wasn't going to be an easy decision, but fortunately she still had months and months before she had to make up her mind.

FOUR

A s she emerged from homeroom the next morning, Callie spotted Stevie strolling down the hall, chatting animatedly with a thin, intense-looking girl named Iris who was in Callie's history class. "Stevie," Callie said, hurrying forward so fast that her crutches almost slipped on the smooth tile floor of the hallway. "Got a second?"

"Hey, Callie," Stevie said cheerfully, watching as Iris wandered off toward class. "Good news. I think I just won over another vote for your brother with my natural wit and charm." She glanced at Callie and did a quick double take when she noticed her expression. "Whoa. What's the matter with you?"

Callie wished she knew the answer to that. She couldn't stop wondering if she'd talked herself into a big mess by agreeing to go to the homecoming dance with George. Why hadn't she just politely told him she was busy for the next two years? He would have gotten the hint, and she wouldn't be faced with a date she wasn't sure she wanted.

She glanced around to make sure nobody else was listening. "It's about George."

Stevie's eyes lit up with curiosity. "Oh?"

"He called me last night, and I told him I'd go to the dance with him tomorrow."

"But that's great!" Stevie exclaimed, giving Callie's arm a quick squeeze. "He really likes you, you know."

"I know." Callie hesitated, not even sure what she wanted to say. "Um, it's just kind of weird. I haven't really gone out with anyone since I moved here, and, well . . ."

Stevie nodded sympathetically. "It must be tough, you know, especially because you're still . . ." She waved her hand at Callie's crutches.

"Well, I guess," Callie said. That wasn't what she'd been thinking about—George had never made her feel the least bit awkward about being on crutches, and besides, her leg was getting stronger every day. With any luck, she'd be as good as new before too long.

Stevie seemed to catch on to what she was thinking. "Anyway," she said, "I'm really glad you're giving him a chance, Callie. A lot of girls look at a guy like George and just see, you know, kind of a quiet, shy guy. But I'm sure there's a whole lot more to him than that."

"You're probably right." Stevie's words made Callie feel a little better. After all, wasn't that really what she was worried about? That George wasn't as cool

48

or as good-looking or as popular as the guys she'd gone out with back in her old hometown? So what? That didn't mean he wasn't worth getting to know. "Thanks, Stevie."

"Anytime." Suddenly Stevie's eyes narrowed as a tall girl with glasses walked past them, surrounded by a group of other students. "Uh-oh. There goes Valerie," she muttered. "I'd better go see what she's talking about."

Callie smiled as Stevie took off after the other students. Valerie Watkins was running against Scott in the school election. From what Callie could tell, Valerie was a smart, thoughtful girl with some good ideas, and she guessed that was why she was the only one of Scott's three opponents that he and Stevie were worried about.

Callie was still smiling as she turned to make her way down the hall to her first class, but suddenly the smile froze on her face. She had just spotted George. He was taking a drink out of the water fountain halfway down the hall. His shirt had come untucked from his slightly rumpled khaki pants, revealing a swath of pasty white skin above a generous portion of white cotton briefs. Callie felt her cheeks grow hot as she quickly looked away, trying not to notice that a couple of freshman girls were pointing at George and giggling behind their hands.

Maybe going to the dance with him isn't such a hot idea, she thought as she hurried in the other direction, not even caring that it meant taking the long way around to her classroom. *I could pretend I'm not feeling well, or come up with some kind of story about family obligations. . . .*

Thinking about her family made her think about her brother. Recalling how she'd climbed on her high horse with Scott the day before, berating him for not considering Veronica's feelings, she realized she was just as bad when it came right down to it. Wasn't she leading George on by agreeing to go out with him when she wasn't sure she could ever like him in a romantic way? Why was she forcing this, anyway? Just because George was interested in her, it didn't mean she had an obligation to go out with him. Why hadn't she turned him down, politely and firmly, the first time he'd approached her?

Because I'm doing what Stevie said, she told herself as she dodged around a crowd of kids emerging from a classroom, nodding at one or two people she knew. *I'm giving the nice guy a chance. Nothing ever worked out with any of the cool guys I knew back home; why pass up a chance to try something different?*

She wasn't quite convinced by her own argument. No matter how many ways she looked at the situation, she wasn't sure she was doing the right thing. She couldn't seem to figure out if she was taking a chance that could turn out to be the smartest thing she'd ever done or making a total idiot of herself for no reason while simultaneously setting up a really sweet guy for a big hurt.

I hate this, she thought fiercely, feeling her hands

clench harder on the grips of her crutches. *There's no way to figure out the right answer. I hate being so wishy-washy!*

Still, she thought there was no way around it. She'd already told George she would go to the dance with him, and the only sure thing she could see was that he would be terribly disappointed—and rightfully so—if she backed out. So the only thing to do was to wait for the next night and see what happened.

Stevie had forgotten about Callie's big date almost as soon as she'd heard about it. She was happy that her friend was giving George a shot, but she had more pressing matters on her mind at the moment than romance. Scott's triumph in arranging the dance the next night was the talk of the school—Miss Fenton had mentioned him by name in her morning announcement as the primary organizer—and Stevie wanted to savor every moment of it. She was still a little worried about Valerie Watkins, especially since she'd been going to Fenton Hall for years and everyone knew she was a major brain, but for today, at least, Scott was the only candidate anyone was talking about. Stevie liked it that way, even if it still irked her that Veronica had been the one who'd helped make it happen.

"Hey, Stevie!" Betsy Cavanaugh cried gleefully, catching her as they were both heading into Señora Johnson's Spanish, their first class of the day.

51

"Check it out. Did you get your ticket yet?" She waved a slip of paper in Stevie's face.

Stevie took a step backward to avoid the danger of a paper cut on her nose. "Not exactly," she told Betsy. "I can't go. I'm grounded, remember?"

Betsy looked perplexed for a moment; then understanding dawned on her face. "Oh, right. The party." She giggled. "Wow, that really bites."

Stevie gritted her teeth and mentally counted to ten, willing herself not to get annoyed. When she trusted herself to speak again, she pasted a bland smile on her face. "Just remember who made this dance possible," she chirped, faking cheeriness. "It was all the work of Scott Forester, the action candidate for student body president. He takes action so you can have fun."

Betsy nodded. "Don't worry, he's got my vote," she promised. She waved her ticket again. "Even if he never does anything else, this is enough!" She giggled and raced past Stevie into the classroom.

Stevie followed more slowly. Everyone was so excited about the dance, and she knew that was a good thing. But it was a little depressing to think that Betsy Cavanaugh and Veronica diAngelo and practically everybody else she knew would be dancing the night away the next evening—while she was home scrubbing toilets and sweeping the garage.

Now I know how Cinderella felt, she thought grumpily as she flopped into her seat, trying to ignore the students around her, who all seemed to be chattering about what they were going to wear to the dance. *Except in my case, there's no chance a fairy godmother is going to come along and rescue me. Because even if she did show up, Mom and Dad would just hand her a mop and put her to work!*

"Yo, Lake!" a senior named Mike Kaminski called as Stevie walked out of her third-period classroom a little later that day. "Tell your action man he's got my vote. This dance is going to rock!" He waved his long arms above his head and swayed to illustrate his point, making the adoring girls who followed him everywhere giggle with delight.

Stevie grinned and gave him a thumbs-up in return. "Thanks, Kaminski. I'll tell him," she promised, trying not to let on how thrilled she was. Mike was one of the most popular guys in school; if he was planning to vote for Scott, a lot of other kids would be sure to follow his lead.

He's probably psyched because his girlfriend goes to Willow Creek, and now all his buddies from the basketball team will be around to keep him company while she's touching up her makeup in the bathroom, she thought.

She noticed that one of Mike's admirers, a pretty, curvaceous junior named Nicole Adams, had stayed behind as the group moved on. She leaned against the wall and pulled out a compact, blinking at herself intently in the tiny mirror.

Stevie decided she might as well do a little more

campaigning while she had the chance. *Nicole may not be the sharpest pencil in the box,* Stevie thought as she strolled toward the other girl, *but she has a lot of friends. Plus,* she added to herself, running her eyes over Nicole's clingy sweater, *most of the guys in this school would do anything she told them to do.*

"Hey, Nicole," Stevie said with a smile. "How's it going?"

Nicole glanced up, looking a little surprised. Stevie didn't blame her—Nicole hung around with the same crowd as Veronica, which meant that she and Stevie had never exactly been close. "Hi," Nicole replied. "It's going, I guess."

"Good." Stevie kept her smile as bright and sincere as she could. "I just wanted to see if you're going to the dance tomorrow night, and if so, to remind you that Scott Forester, the action candidate for student body president, was the one who made it all possible."

"Uh-huh." Nicole nodded absently, having returned her attention to her compact mirror as Stevie spoke.

Stevie wasn't finished. "I also thought you might want to know that Scott has other big plans for our school. Plans that will make your life better. For instance, he wants to hold a separate fund-raiser for the junior-senior trip so that more students will be able to go."

Nicole looked up from her mirror and blinked. "I know," she said, tossing her shoulder-length, wavy blond hair and smiling as several of her friends walked by and waved to her. "Veronica already told me all about that days ago. Actually, she said Scott might try to convince Miss Fenton to let us go to Tahiti this year."

Stevie held back a snort. She was sure that Scott had said no such thing. It sounded like vintage Veronica to her. "Well, maybe," she said as diplomatically as she could. "Anyway, I hope you'll remember Scott on Election Day next week."

"Yeah, whatever." Nicole had clearly lost interest in the conversation. Snapping her compact shut and shoving it into her purse, she headed off down the hall without a backward glance.

Stevie rolled her eyes and let her go. *It figures,* she thought sourly. *Veronica already thinks she's Scott's campaign manager. Pretty soon she'll probably start thinking she's running for office herself.* Glancing at her watch, she realized she only had a few minutes to get upstairs to her fourth-period English lit class. She headed down the crowded hall, wondering if it would hurt Scott's election chances if his campaign manager were to murder Veronica diAngelo.

Still, she couldn't resist the urge to do a little more campaigning as she went. With the election only four days away, every minute counted—especially when it came to the students who might not even bother to go to the dance over the weekend. As she made her way toward the stairs at the end of the hall, Stevie passed Zach Lincoln, a nerdy, angular boy with an uneven haircut and a slight tic above his left eye that had earned him the nickname Blinkin' Lincoln in elementary school. Ignoring his twitching forehead, Stevie grabbed his arm. "Hi, Zach," she said in her friendliest tone. "What's new?"

Zach cast her a suspicious glance. "How about you talking to me?" he replied.

Stevie laughed as if he'd actually said something witty. "Good one," she said. "But listen, I just wanted to talk to you about Scott Forester, the action candidate for student body president . . ." She plunged into her usual speech, mentioning the dance briefly and then moving on to describe the trip fundraiser idea as well as Scott's plans to update the software in the school computer lab.

"Yeah, yeah." Zach cut her off before she could finish. "I heard all about it. The action candidate, man of action, blah blah blah. I've got it. Veronica talked my ear off about it in homeroom."

Stevie's jaw dropped, and for a second she couldn't respond. She shouldn't have been surprised that Veronica had been spouting off to friends like Nicole about all her big plans for Scott's presidency. But Zach Lincoln? Stevie doubted Veronica had ever spoken to him before in her entire life, unless it was to taunt him.

"Oh, okay then," she said, trying to be patient. "Did you know that Scott also intends to distribute a survey once he's elected to find out what issues matter to you?"

"Uh-huh." Zach looked at her as if she'd suddenly grown three or four extra heads. "Veronica told me that, too. Don't you guys talk to each other? I thought you political manager types were supposed to be so organized."

"Yeah," Stevie snapped, not even caring if Zach thought she was obnoxious. "We held a secret summit meeting and agreed to make sure we told everybody in school the same thing at least twice. After that, we're going to get to work on taking over the world and creating a benevolent dictatorship." She stalked away, leaving Zach staring after her.

I'm *supposed to be Scott's campaign manager,* she fumed as she strode toward the stairs. Thanks to her fruitless little chat with Zach, she was probably going to be late for English lit. *He asked me, and only me. So where does Veronica get off electing herself to share the job?*

In the cafeteria a little while later, Stevie was telling the students standing near her in the lunch line about all the plans Scott had for the marching band's budget problems, when she felt a hand on her arm. "I couldn't help overhearing," Veronica diAngelo said smoothly, inserting herself into the center of the group before Stevie quite realized what was happening. "I thought you all might like to know the latest. I was having a private talk with the candidate just before lunch, and he told me he really wants this year to be special here at Fenton Hall. That's why he came up with his latest plan." She paused and glanced around, making sure that everyone was hanging on her every word.

Stevie shot her a suspicious glare, wondering what she was up to. As far as she knew, Scott hadn't come up with any fabulous new plans, although she had to admit she hadn't spoken to him much that day.

"What are you talking about, Veronica?" she asked sharply. "I was already telling them about how the cost of the new band uniforms is—"

"Is totally boring," Veronica interrupted with a smile for her audience. She shrugged and casually ran her fingers through the ends of her shiny dark hair. "I don't know how you guys feel about it, but I'm not really that interested in all that budget stuff."

Stevie gritted her teeth. It took all her self-control not to tell Veronica off right then and there. But, she reminded herself, it wouldn't make Scott look very good if his campaign manager blew up at his supposed girlfriend.

Veronica didn't even seem to notice Stevie's consternation. Her pretty, high-cheekboned face still held that self-satisfied smile. "One thing I do care about, though," she said, "is where we're going to have our prom this spring. I mean, the public high school holds theirs at the Creekside Hotel every year—it's ridiculous that ours is always right here in the stinky old Fenton Hall gym. That's why Scott has promised that this year, ours will take place in the ballroom of the Willow Creek Country Club." She paused just long enough to let what she'd said sink in. "Scott and I think that would be a *much* more romantic place for the prom."

Of course you do, Stevie thought bitterly. *Your parents practically own the place. But remember, the hard part will be convincing Miss Fenton, the queen of tradition, to change the way we've always done things.*

She opened her mouth to explain that she was sure all Scott was really doing was discussing options for the prom—after all, it was still months away. But it was too late. The other students were already chattering excitedly about Veronica's announcement.

Stevie was still brooding about Veronica's outrageous comments as she grabbed her American history textbook out of her locker just before last period. Her mood had been swinging all day between elation at Scott's blossoming popularity and annoyance at the way Veronica kept trying to insinuate herself into the campaign. But the closer the dance loomed, the more she simply found herself wishing that she could go to it instead of staying home and working her fingers to the bone.

Why was I so stupid last weekend? she wondered helplessly. *If only I hadn't taken that first sip of beer . . . I'm sure Mom and Dad would have been a lot more forgiving about the mess and everything if—*

"Stevie." A familiar voice broke into her thoughts. "Earth to Stevie."

"Scott!" Stevie slammed her locker shut and grabbed him by the arm. "Listen, do you have any idea what Veronica's telling people now?" She paused and peered at him more closely, noticing that his usual friendly, jovial expression had been replaced by a more somber, thoughtful look. "What's the matter with you?"

Scott ran a hand through his hair and glanced from side to side. "I want to ask you about something," he said. "Come on, let's duck in there for a minute." He nodded to an empty classroom across the hall.

Stevie followed, feeling worried. As soon as they were alone, she turned to him with her hands on her hips. "What's the problem?" she demanded, knowing there was no time to beat around the bush. Her history class started in less than five minutes. "Does this have something to do with Veronica and the prom?"

"Prom, no. Veronica, yes." Scott leaned against the edge of the teacher's desk and furrowed his brow. "Callie started me thinking yesterday, and well, now I'm just not sure what I should do."

"What do you mean?" Stevie wasn't following him. "Do about what?"

Scott shrugged. "Veronica, of course."

"Well, unfortunately, murder's against the law," Stevie said tartly, tapping one foot impatiently against the hard tile floor. "Otherwise, the solution would be simple. I understand that they're working

60

on personality transplants, but you know how slow the FDA is. . . ."

Scott smiled, but it looked a bit forced. "No, really," he insisted. "I don't have much time. I mean, if I don't ask her to the dance soon, she'll probably ask me—she's been dropping some pretty obvious hints as it is—and then I'll have to figure out what to tell her, and no matter what I say—"

"Wait a minute." Stevie held up a hand to stop him, struggling to catch up. "This is about asking her to the dance? What, did you suddenly come down with a case of shyness?" She shook her head in confusion. "I assumed you'd already asked her. She's certainly acting as though you two are a couple." She couldn't help shuddering slightly at the very idea.

"But that's just it." Scott spread his hands out before him helplessly. "I haven't asked her. I don't really want to ask her. But if I don't, what will people think?"

"They'll probably think you have some taste," Stevie replied. Then she paused. "Wait a minute. Did I just hear you right? You *don't* want to ask her? Then why have you been letting her think you're into her?"

Scott looked sheepish. "I guess I didn't realize that's what I was doing," he admitted, picking at the pockmarked surface of the desk. "Not until Callie said something yesterday. She doesn't think it'll look good if I take Ronnie to the dance and then tell her I don't want to get serious. It'll look like I was using her all along. You know, for her family connections or whatever." He shrugged. "I don't want people thinking that about me, and I certainly don't want to lead her on."

Stevie blew out a noisy sigh. "Oh, wow," she said blankly. "This is a hell of a time to start thinking about this. Why couldn't you have just blown her off when she first started hanging around and batting her eyelashes at you?"

Scott shrugged again, not quite meeting her eye. "I think she's an interesting person. And, you know, attractive. I kind of like hanging out with her. I'm just not interested in getting involved in some kind of romantic relationship with her right now."

I get it, Stevie thought, feeling a bit frustrated with him. *You kind of like hanging out with her, because you kind of like having pretty girls following you around, hanging on your every word. Unfortunately, you misjudged this particular girl in a big way, and she's probably going to make you pay for it.*

Still, she couldn't help feeling a twinge of satisfaction that Veronica's charms hadn't won Scott over. Veronica wasn't used to being rejected by guys—Stevie would love to see her face when Scott blew her off. . . .

But she stopped herself from that line of thought. This was no time to be thinking of her own personal entertainment. She had to be practical—they had an election to win.

"Listen," she told Scott, going over and perching

beside him on the desk. She was so busy trying to figure out how to phrase what she wanted to say next that she hardly noticed as the bell rang, signaling that she was officially late for history class. "I hear what you're saying. But I really think you're making too big a deal of this. I mean, Veronica goes through boyfriends like most people go through candy bars. So you might as well make things easy for yourself and just take her to the dance."

Scott was already shaking his head by the time she finished. "I don't want to be like that," he said stubbornly. "I'm not that kind of guy."

Stevie gritted her teeth, tempted to grab him and shake him. "Look, I don't like giving this advice any more than you like hearing it," she told him bluntly. "But you've got to be realistic about this. You know that saying about the fury of a woman scorned, or whatever?" She scowled. "Well, it was practically invented for Veronica. If you tell her you're not interested, she'll make your life miserable. It's just not worth it, especially now, so close to the election."

"I see where you're coming from," Scott said. "But I'm not going to pretend to have feelings for her when I don't."

Stevie raked her hands through her hair. "I know, I know!" she exclaimed. "I'm not saying you have to propose or anything. I mean, come on—I'm the last person who's going to say you ought to *like* that stuck-up snake. But can't you just play along a little longer? If you really don't want to take her to the dance, maybe you could come up with an excuse, like saying you need to be free to concentrate on campaigning or something." She shrugged. "But if that doesn't satisfy, you may need to just go out with her this once. You can figure out how to deal with it after you're president, if a miracle occurs and she doesn't get bored with you by then." She winced as she said it, feeling more like Cinderella than ever as she pictured smug Veronica holding court at the dance by Scott's side while Stevie slaved away at her endless chores at home.

Scott stood up and nodded. "Thanks for your input, Stevie," he said, glancing at his watch. "Sorry, I've made you late. I forgot not everyone has a study hall this period."

"Don't worry about it." Stevie stood, too, trying to get a look at Scott's expression. He was a good six inches taller than she, so it was hard for her to see his eyes. "So what are you going to do?" she asked cautiously.

"I have to do what I think is right." He finally looked Stevie in the eye, and her heart sank when she saw the determined set of his jaw. "I don't want people getting the idea that I'm some kind of user. I shouldn't have let things get this far with Veronica." He nodded firmly. "I'm going to talk to her right after school, let her know where things stand with us."

"But Scott—"

He cut her off before she could say anything

more. "My mind is made up, Stevie," he said. "Callie's right—I've got to do something about this right away."

Oh, Callie, Stevie thought desperately as she followed him out of the empty classroom. *Why did you have to speak up about this now of all times?*

She was sure that Callie had meant well. Maybe she would even be right—*if* they were dealing with anyone but Veronica diAngelo. The Foresters were still new enough to Fenton Hall that they didn't know how vindictive she could be when she thought she'd been wronged.

As Stevie hurried through the silent halls toward her history classroom, she knew she ought to start figuring out what she was going to say to Mr. Carpenter to explain her tardiness. Instead, all she could think about was Scott's decision.

Crossing her fingers, she decided that all she could do was hope for the best and see what happened. *I don't know what good that will do, though,* she thought ruefully, staring down at her crossed fingers. *My luck hasn't exactly been the greatest lately.*

FIVE

Wow, Carole thought at the beginning of her seventh-period class. *This must be my lucky day!* She could hardly contain her joy as she stared at the quiz her history teacher had just returned, particularly the big *A—95%* written in bold red ink at the top of the page.

"Nice work, Carole," Ms. Shepard said quietly, pausing on her way back up the aisle after distributing other students' papers. She patted Carole on the shoulder. "You've really turned things around in the past few weeks. This quiz brings you up to a solid B-plus for the semester."

"Thanks," Carole replied softly. She glanced at the grade again as the teacher moved on. She knew she deserved the A—she'd read this week's assignment three or four times in study hall.

Still, she found herself quickly folding the paper in half and stuffing it into her backpack. She was starting to wonder if she would ever be able to simply enjoy a good grade again after what she'd done. Several weeks had passed since the day she'd given in to temptation and cheated on a history test, but her feelings of guilt hadn't ebbed much in that time. Whenever she thought about how she'd peeked in her textbook when the teacher was out of the room, she felt her face grow hot with shame.

At least nobody ever has to know, she told herself, but that thought wasn't much comfort. She knew she would have been in big trouble if she'd been caught. But not being caught seemed almost as bad, because it meant she had to live with the knowledge of what she'd done all by herself, with no one to help her through it.

Carole wasn't used to keeping secrets from the people she loved—she and her father had been close ever since the death of her mother years earlier, and it felt horrible to keep something so major from him. Then there were her friends. Until the test, there had never been anything she'd felt she had to hide from Stevie and Lisa. But this was different. It could change the whole way they thought about her, and she definitely didn't want to risk that.

I really didn't have a choice, though, she thought helplessly. *If I'd failed that test, my average would have fallen way below a C. That means Max would have banished me from Pine Hollow until I brought the grade up. Plus Dad would have been so disappointed— he probably would have chained me to my desk until I memorized the entire history of the world.*

She slouched in her seat and gnawed on her lower lip, hardly hearing as her teacher started reviewing the quiz. Thinking about how she'd tricked the people she cared about still hurt, no matter how certain she was that she'd only done what she'd had to do.

There's one more thing I need to remember, she told herself firmly. *If I'd let that grade slip, I wouldn't be getting ready to ride Samson at Colesford right now. That's got to be worth all this guilt and then some.*

That thought made her sit up straight at her desk. No matter how guilty she felt about what she'd done, she couldn't imagine how horrible she would have felt if she'd blown the chance to take Samson to the big show.

Stevie's comments the day before floated uninvited through her mind. Carole still wasn't sure what to think of her friend's remark, but she knew that at least part of it was true. She really did love spending every possible minute with the big black horse. They made a great team—obviously Max had seen that, since he'd asked her to ride Samson at Colesford. Stevie had seen it. Even Ben seemed to have noticed, though she still wasn't sure what he'd been driving at the day before during that awkward almost-conversation in the stable aisle.

Knowing that she'd done what she'd done at least partially for Samson didn't make everything totally better, of course—only more time would do that, if she was lucky. But at least it gave her something else to think about.

She smiled slightly and shifted her thoughts to the jump course she planned to set up for Samson's training session that afternoon. Settling back in her seat once again, she started running possible combinations through her mind as her teacher's voice faded slowly away.

Stevie glanced at her watch for the fourth time. "Come on, Alex," she muttered impatiently under her breath. "Some of us have ovens to clean, you know."

She leaned against the hood of the small two-door car that she and Alex shared and crossed her arms over her chest. Kicking at a stone on the cracked asphalt of the student parking lot, she decided she'd give him five more minutes before she left without him. For all she knew, he might have spaced out and gone home on the bus or caught a ride with friends.

As she was trying to figure out what new horrors her parents would come up with to punish her twin if he forgot he was grounded, she heard a sudden commotion from several cars down. Turning idly to see what was going on, she gulped as she saw Scott and Veronica facing off beside Scott's green sports car. Veronica's eyes were blazing, and she was yelling something about two-faced weasels—Stevie couldn't quite make out the rest of the insult.

"Uh-oh," Stevie whispered. She eased around the back of her own car, trying to get close enough to hear them without being noticed. She needn't have worried. Veronica and Scott were so caught up in their conversation that they never even glanced her way.

". . . and so after all we've been through together, you have the nerve to tell me you just want to be friends?" Veronica shrieked furiously. She slammed her designer handbag down on the hood of Scott's car so hard that it snapped open and a couple of lipsticks and a gold-trimmed compact flew out. "I can't believe this!"

Scott dropped to his knees and frantically started collecting the spilled items. "Please, Ronnie," he said. "I'm sorry. Don't take this the wrong way. I think you're great. It's just—"

"It's just that you were using me, and now that you've got everything you want, you're finished." Veronica folded her arms over her chest and stared at him icily, ignoring the retrieved makeup in his outstretched hands. "Well, maybe you could get away with that sort of thing back in your old school, but you're not going to get away with it with me."

"Listen, Ronnie," Scott said, laying the makeup on the hood of his car and touching her arm. "I'm really sorry about the timing here. If you're upset about the dance—I mean, if you were counting on me, I guess we could still—"

Stevie cringed on Scott's behalf as Veronica's eyes opened wide in disbelief. *Talk about saying the wrong thing,* she thought ruefully.

"Don't do me any favors," Veronica snapped contemptuously, cutting Scott off in midsentence. "I don't need your stupid charity date. I don't need you at all." She whirled and started to storm away. But then she paused and looked back at him, her angry expression fading slightly and a crafty gleam coming into her eyes. "Of course, that doesn't necessarily go both ways," she said enigmatically before turning and stomping away.

"Ronnie, wait," Scott called after her anxiously. "I'm sorry. Can't we talk about this?" He hurried after her.

"Hey, sis. What's going on?"

Stevie turned and saw that her brother had just wandered up and was gazing after Scott curiously. "You missed it," she said. "Scott just—well, I guess you could say he broke up with Veronica."

Alex whistled. "Wow."

"No kidding. Needless to say, she didn't take it well." Stevie rubbed her ear, feeling worried. "I'm afraid she's going to take some horrible revenge on Scott. You know, like paying every student at Fenton Hall a hundred dollars to vote for someone else on Tuesday, or—"

"Don't worry," Alex interrupted. He walked around to the passenger's side of their car and opened the door. "Scott's a big boy. He can handle it."

Stevie shot him a surprised look through the driver's side window. Opening the door, she slid inside and fished for the seat belt, which was forever getting stuck beneath the seat. "Gee, do you think you could be a little *less* sympathetic? This is a major crisis here."

"Sorry." Alex sighed and ran a hand over his face, looking tired. "I know you're really into this election thing, but to be honest, I've got other stuff on my mind."

Stevie fished the car keys out of her pocket. "Like what? I'm grounded too, remember."

"It's not that." Alex shot her a sidelong glance. "It's just, you know . . ."

"Oh." Suddenly Stevie realized that he must be thinking about Lisa. She knew it had been really hard on him to discover that Lisa had been hiding the truth from him about her talk with Skye. "Look," she said matter-of-factly as she gunned the ignition. "You've got to get over this. I know she wasn't totally honest with you, but it's not like you were much help. Everyone knows how much you hated her going to California in the first place, and how jealous you've always been of her friendship with Skye."

"I know, I know." Alex sighed and propped one foot on the dashboard as Stevie pulled out of the parking lot. "I just can't help it, you know? I mean, I really, really want to make things work with us. But it's like whenever I'm with her now, I can't stop thinking about"—he grimaced slightly—"you know, *him*. I can't help imagining how much time they spent together this summer and how he was probably hoping to win her over the whole time.

And now she's going back there for Thanksgiving. . . ." His voice trailed off, and he lifted his hands helplessly for a moment before letting them fall limply back onto the seat.

Stevie sighed impatiently, wishing that everyone she knew could just step back and get some perspective, see what they were doing wrong. "I've said it before and I'll say it again," she told her brother. "You've just got to get over it. The important thing is that you two want to be together. Right?"

"I guess," Alex agreed reluctantly. "But how does that help me, really? I still hate the fact that she keeps going off to California without me. I know it upsets her that I feel that way, but it's the way I honestly feel, you know? How can she expect me to change that?"

Stevie didn't know how to answer him. And just at the moment she didn't want to spend time trying to figure it out.

I'm sure he and Lisa will work things out somehow, she thought, glancing over at her twin, who was slumped against the car door staring moodily out the window. She returned her own gaze to the road, clutching the wheel tightly as her thoughts strayed back to the problem occupying her own mind. *Scott and Veronica, on the other hand . . .*

SIX

Later that evening Stevie walked into the kitchen and found her mother sitting at the table reading the newspaper. "The bathroom is so clean you could perform surgery on the floor and sterilize your scalpels in the toilet," Stevie announced wearily, pushing a sweaty strand of hair out of her eyes before she remembered she was still wearing rubber gloves. Peeling them off, she tossed them in the general direction of the kitchen sink. "Is it okay if I call Phil now?"

Mrs. Lake gave her an appraising glance. "I suppose so," she agreed. "But don't talk longer than ten minutes. You're grounded, remember?"

"How could I forget?" Stevie muttered under her breath as she left the kitchen and headed for the stairs. When her mother cocked a warning eyebrow in her direction, Stevie forced a weak smile. "I mean, thanks, Mom. Ten minutes. Got it."

Soon she was sitting on the edge of her bed with the phone in her hand. She quickly dialed Phil's number, suddenly realizing how eager she was to hear his voice. He went to a different school in a town a few miles from Willow Creek, which meant that because of her grounding, she hadn't seen him since the party.

"Hello?" he answered a moment later.

"Hi, it's me," she said, settling back against her pillow. "What's up?"

"Hey, Stevie." He sounded so happy to hear from her that she felt better immediately. "How's life on the chain gang?"

"Disgusting," she said. "I'm now more intimately acquainted with all the toilets in this house than I ever thought was possible."

His familiar laughter bubbled through the phone. "Tough break," he said. "But think of it this way. At least after this you'll have a marketable job skill. The world will always need its toilets cleaned."

Stevie grimaced. Phil had been grounded because of the party, too—thanks to Stevie's encouragement, he'd had several beers and ended up being driven home by the police. But his parents had set his punishment at a measly two weeks. "Very funny," she said. "You'd better watch it, or once you're sprung I'll expect you to come over and help me."

"Sounds good to me," Phil replied quickly. "I'm willing to clean as many toilets as it takes, as long as it means we can be together. I miss you, you know."

Stevie smiled, pleased at the compliment. But she couldn't concentrate on Phil's romantic words for long. She only had ten minutes to talk, and she really wanted to get a few things off her chest before she exploded. "Me too," she said quickly. "But listen, I can't talk long. And you'll never guess what happened at school today."

"What?"

"Get this." Stevie snuggled down deeper into her pillow and switched the phone to her other ear. "Scott broke up with Veronica."

"Were they actually going out?"

"That was the problem." Stevie smiled grimly. "She thought they were. He thought they weren't."

"Uh-oh," Phil said. "So listen, do you think your parents would count shopping as a date? Because I need some new shoes, and I was hoping—"

"Forget it." Stevie cut him off. "I'm chained to the house for the next decade at least. But anyway, like I was saying, Scott suddenly decided to turn into Mr. Straight Up and tell Veronica they weren't going to happen. So now she's mad, and you know what Veronica's like when she's mad."

"Psychotic," Phil said helpfully. "Vengeful. Uh, malevolent?"

Stevie grinned. She recognized the last two words from the PSAT vocabulary list she and Phil had studied earlier that fall. "Right," she agreed. "So now I'm afraid she might try to mess up the election somehow. Maybe try to make Scott look bad at the dance or something like that."

"Of course," Phil said.

"That's why it really sucks that I'm not going."

Stevie bit her lip and stared at her bedroom ceiling. "I wish I could be there to keep an eye on Scott."

Phil cleared his throat. "I'm sure Scott can deal," he said. "He strikes me as the kind of guy who can take care of himself."

"Maybe," Stevie agreed. "But then again, Veronica *is* Veronica. And Scott can be kind of easily distracted sometimes. It would be better if I could be there, you know, to keep him on track." She tapped her fingers restlessly on the phone. "That's why I need to find someone who's going tomorrow night. Someone I can count on to watch out for him."

"Hey, you know I'd help you out if we were still going," Phil said. "Especially if part of our spy cover was that we had to make out so nobody would think we were watching them."

"Yeah, big help," Stevie muttered. "Anyway, that's the problem. Hardly anyone I would trust with this job is going. Alex is grounded too, of course, so he's out. And Lisa won't even think of going to the dance without him." She sighed. "I tried to talk Carole into it when I saw her at Pine Hollow this afternoon, but I can already tell that's a lost cause. She wants to spend every possible second preparing for the horse show. I doubt she even remembered there was a dance until I reminded her."

"That's Carole for you," Phil said lightly. "One-track mind."

"Tell me about it." Stevie frowned at the ceiling. "I was thinking about getting Callie involved. After

77

all, this is sort of her fault—apparently she was the one who gave Scott the idea to ditch Veronica. But she's got that date with George. I don't want to get in the way of that, you know?"

"Right. God forbid you should stand in the way of romance."

Stevie noticed that Phil sounded a bit odd. But she dismissed the thought, figuring she was probably imagining it. Worrying about what Veronica would do next could make anyone a little paranoid. "So what do you think I should do?"

"I think you should take your mind off it by whispering sweet nothings in my ear," Phil said. "It won't be the same over the phone as in person, but—"

"Come on," Stevie said, starting to feel a little annoyed with him. He didn't even seem to care about her problem. "This is serious."

"So am I," Phil insisted. "Seriously wishing you weren't grounded so we could meet at the park. You know, settle down in our favorite spot under that tree . . ."

Stevie sighed. Obviously Phil wasn't going to be any help—all he could seem to focus on was making out and complaining about her being grounded. "Uh-huh. Listen, I think I hear Mom calling me," she lied. "Guess that means my time's up. I'll call you tomorrow, okay?"

"Okay. Love ya."

"Back at you," she said automatically. Then she

hung up, rolled onto her back on the bed again, and rubbed her face dejectedly. Why didn't anyone seem to care that her whole campaign could be going up in smoke?

"Hold still, boy," Carole murmured, moving with Starlight as he shifted from side to side, tossing his head. With her lower lip clamped in her teeth, she made a grab for the girth, which was swinging crazily beneath the horse's belly because of his antics. Finally she caught it and began to fasten it. "There we go," she told the tall bay gelding as soothingly as she could. "Just a minute and we'll be ready to go, okay?"

The horse turned his head to look at her, stamping one hind foot impatiently. Carole gave him an apologetic pat, then returned to her task, pulling the girth tight after smoothing the glossy mahogany hair lying beneath it.

As she reached for the bridle, she made a move to check the time. Her wrist was bare, and she remembered she'd removed her watch a little while earlier when she was giving Samson a bath. She smiled automatically at the thought of that day's workout with the big black horse, which had gone very well, as usual.

But then her smile faded, and she sighed. *What's wrong with me?* she wondered as she buckled the throatlatch on Starlight's bridle. He shook his head again, almost bonking her on the head with his nose, and she shoved him away a little more roughly than necessary. She blinked, feeling guilty and annoyed and out of sorts. *What's my problem today?* Her weird mood had been building all afternoon, ever since she'd arrived at Pine Hollow. There wasn't any good reason for it as far as she could tell—her chores had gone smoothly, there hadn't been any big lesson groups that day to cause a hassle, Samson was in great shape, the other horses were all healthy. . . .

"All I can say is, I'd better not be coming down with something," she told Starlight as she finished buckling his bridle. "I don't have time to get sick right now."

She shuddered at the very thought, imagining lying home in bed while Stevie and Ben and the others went off to Colesford without her. But she didn't really think she was getting sick—aside from being a bit tired from her busy schedule, she felt just fine. Physically, at least.

I'm probably just feeling grumpy because I'm hungry, she told herself, leading Starlight out of his stall. It was getting late, so she headed toward the well-lighted indoor ring, planning to exercise him over the small jump course Max had set up for a private lesson earlier that day. *I guess an apple and a piece of cheese doesn't really make much of a dinner.* Her father was attending a charity event in Washington, D.C., that evening, so Carole hadn't bothered to go home to eat.

Of course, this wasn't the first time she'd skipped

a meal when she was busy at the stable. And it had never made her feel this way before—unsettled and almost depressed, as if she might start weeping if she didn't watch herself.

She took a few deep breaths as she and Starlight turned the corner at the end of the aisle, hoping that would calm her down. But she couldn't seem to banish the weird, dejected feelings that continued their melancholy dance somewhere deep inside her.

It's probably because of what happened in history class today, she thought. *I'm still feeling guilty about that test. I guess maybe I always will.*

But that explanation didn't quite satisfy her, either. It was true that she'd been plagued by thoughts of her cheating ever since it had happened. Those thoughts had even intruded on her work at the stable from time to time. But never like this. Never giving her the creeping, ominous feeling that her world might be ending.

The heavy wooden doors of the indoor ring were propped open, so she led Starlight inside without delay, heading for the mounting block to one side of the entrance. She wondered if everything that had happened at the party the weekend before was finally catching up with her. It had been an emotional evening—she'd accidentally betrayed one of her best friends, watched the resulting breakup of a couple she had never ever seen fight before, witnessed several of her close friends getting drunk and acting totally different than usual, made a complete fool of herself in front of Ben. . . .

She still shuddered at the thought of everything that had happened that night. But once again, none of it seemed adequate to explain her current mood. Realizing that she'd walked right past the mounting block, still leading Starlight, she turned and retraced her steps, feeling foolish.

As they reached the block again, she glanced at her horse. He stared back at her placidly, waiting for her to go through the familiar motions of climbing into his saddle the way she'd done hundreds, maybe thousands, of times before.

"Ready, boy?" Carole asked the horse, running her hand down his neck. She gulped as a sudden wave of sadness washed over her. Shaking her head to clear it, she gazed at Starlight as another explanation for her weird mood dawned on her.

Maybe that's what's bothering me, she thought. *Maybe it's what Stevie said. Maybe I really have moved on without realizing it—outgrown Starlight when I wasn't even paying attention. Maybe I'm just starting to see that he doesn't fulfill me anymore, at least not the way a horse like Samson could. . . .*

She shook her head again, more fiercely this time. "Don't be stupid," she muttered to herself angrily. She wondered if she was even more tired than she'd thought—why else would she be thinking such crazy, melodramatic thoughts? Stepping onto the mounting block, she stuck her left foot into the stirrup and swung herself aboard. The motion felt familiar and automatic, though somehow less comforting than usual.

Doing her best to push everything else to the back of her mind, she concentrated on her horse. He hadn't been getting enough exercise lately, she realized. Even though it was getting late, she vowed to give him a nice long workout. Beginning at a walk to stretch his long legs, she sent him around the ring.

She settled into the rhythm of the pace, her mind wandering back to the very first time she'd ever ridden Starlight. He hadn't belonged to her then—she hadn't even known that her father was thinking of buying her a horse that Christmas. Still, she'd felt something special about the young gelding. Looking back, it was almost as if some inner part of her had known that they were meant to be together, even though her outer self had no idea such a thing was possible.

That's why it's crazy even to think that Starlight might not be the horse for me anymore, she told herself as she signaled for a trot and her horse responded immediately, shifting to the smooth, swinging gait that she had always loved.

Now that she'd started thinking about the past, she couldn't seem to stop. She remembered all the shows she and Starlight had competed in together. None of them had been nearly as prestigious as Colesford, of course, but each of them had taught her a lot about riding and competing. She had a whole wall full of ribbons and trophies to prove it.

She knew she deserved every one of them, too. Starlight had been quite young when she'd gotten him, but he had been smart and willing, and that, combined with her diligent work over the years, had turned him into a wonderfully responsive, well-trained mount. Training Starlight had taught her even more than competing with him had.

Of course, it hadn't all been about teaching and learning and working. She'd had a lot of fun with her horse over the years, too. They'd played countless gymkhana games, covered innumerable miles of trails behind Pine Hollow, even gone on a foxhunt or two. Thinking back, it was hard for Carole to remember when she and Starlight hadn't been a team.

She smiled, feeling a little better. Her weird mood would pass. In the meantime, she had some riding to do. Quashing her nostalgic thoughts and everything else that was rolling around in her head, she threw herself into the exercise session.

It was quite late by the time Carole finished putting Starlight through his paces, and when she emerged from the indoor ring she found that the stable was almost deserted. Starlight's hoofbeats echoed softly as they walked down the aisle to his stall, and even most of the horses seemed too sleepy to care as they walked by. She slung his sweaty tack over the stall door and gave him a quick grooming, too tired to think anymore about anything but getting home and collapsing into bed.

But first she had some tack to clean. One of Max's strictest rules was that riders had to clean the saddles and bridles they used right away to keep them in good condition. "Okay, boy," Carole told Starlight wearily, dropping her grooming tools back into their bucket. "That's it for today." She gave him a pat, and he nudged at her with his warm, soft nose, snorting softly into her shirt.

She smiled and scratched him in his favorite spot, leaning against his comforting bulk. After a moment he turned away to snuffle at his water bucket, blowing droplets everywhere as he always did before settling down to drink. Carole smiled again, watching him for a moment before letting herself out of the stall and picking up the tack.

Carole had always enjoyed being the only human in a stable full of horses, and she walked slowly toward the tack room, savoring the feeling. There was a whole different mood in the place at this hour—a peaceful, sleepy, serene sensibility that was a contrast to the usual bustling, noisy level of daytime activity.

Still, as she walked along, some of her earlier discontent returned, lapping gently at the corners of her mind. She willed herself not to let it in, telling herself it was just a mood, not worth analyzing and worrying about. But she found her steps coming more rapidly, as if she could leave her weird feelings behind, perhaps somewhere back by Starlight's stall. . . .

She was moving briskly by the time she reached the tack room and took the turn into the open doorway. But she stopped short, a small, startled cry escaping from her lips as she realized she wasn't alone in the stable after all.

Ben looked up from the bit he was polishing. Only one of the overhead lights was on, and his eyes were hidden in shadow as he looked at her and nodded. "Hi," he said, not seeming the least bit surprised to see her.

She swallowed back her own surprise and returned his greeting. "What are you doing here so late?" she asked. "I thought everyone had gone home."

"Catching up," Ben explained, holding up the bit. Then he lapsed into silence as Carole made her way over to a saddle rack and set Starlight's saddle on it. As she hung her bridle on the hook above it, she cast a quick glance at Ben out of the corner of her eye. All his attention seemed to be focused once again on his task as he wiped the bit carefully. But as she was watching him, he suddenly looked up and met her eye.

She gulped and forced a smile, then turned away and busied herself with the dirty bridle. The last thing she wanted was for Ben to think she was staring at him. For one thing, he was such a private, guarded person that he would probably take it as an insult, or he'd think that she wanted to pry into his life. Besides, she still hadn't quite managed to forget about that humiliating misunderstanding at the party. And she certainly didn't want him to guess that she was still thinking about it. . . .

"Carole."

She turned quickly, her heart in her throat, suddenly and irrationally certain that he'd read her mind. He was leaning forward, looking at her.

"Um, yes?"

He held up his hand, and Carole saw her watch dangling from his fingers. "Yours?"

"Thanks. I almost forgot about that." Carole reached for the watch, her hand lightly brushing his as she took it and making her suddenly feel more awkward than ever about being there with him, all alone, late at night. . . .

Get a grip, girl, she told herself, annoyed at her own jumpiness. She turned away to buckle the watch back on. *It's not like this is any big deal. It's not like it would ever occur to him that there was any difference between us being here now, by ourselves, and being here in the middle of the day with a million other people around.*

When she was sure she'd gotten herself back under control, she turned back to him with a grateful smile. "Thanks again," she said. "I took it off when I was getting ready to give Samson his bath earlier, and I stuck it in here so I'd be sure to see it on my way out. But after the busy day I've had, I probably would have totally—"

"Carole," Ben interrupted. She realized he was watching her, his hands and the half-polished bit resting in his lap. "I want—uh, that is—"

"What is it?" Carole's heart leaped to her throat, though she wasn't sure why.

Ben cleared his throat. His eyes wandered from her face to the wall behind her, and then to his own hands, still in his lap. "I don't like to—well, I like to leave people alone," he said slowly. "But I've been thinking."

There was a long pause, and Carole suddenly remembered how Ben had seemed to want to tell her something the previous day, before Max had come along and interrupted them. "Is this—does this have something to do with Samson?" she asked uncertainly. "I mean, yesterday you started to say—"

Ben nodded curtly. "Samson." His eyes flicked back to her face. "You and Samson. I've noticed, well . . . you're pretty wrapped up in him."

"Yeah?" Carole frowned slightly. Ben had said something to that effect to her a couple of weeks earlier. At the time, she'd thought he was implying that she wasn't carrying her weight around the stable because she was spending too much time on Samson's training. But suddenly she wasn't sure that was what he'd been saying at all. "Uh, I mean, yeah," she said. "I guess I have been working with him a lot lately. But, you know, the show . . ."

"Right." Ben grimaced. "But it's not just that."

He didn't seem inclined to go on at first. His eyes had returned to his hands, and he was staring at them thoughtfully, shadows once again obscuring his expression. "Yes?" Carole prompted after a few seconds of silence. "Um, I mean, is there something else?"

He glanced at her; his dark eyes looked startled and a bit wary, as if he were trying to figure out what to say next. "Starlight," he said succinctly. "What about Starlight?"

Carole gasped, her earlier thoughts flooding back in a rush. "What about him?" she asked in a tiny, strangled voice, clutching the saddle rack beside her for support.

Ben shrugged, still watching her carefully. "Have you been thinking much about him? Since, you know, Samson came?"

"Sure," Carole said quickly. But then she stopped herself. "Uh, sort of, I guess. What do you mean?" Ben was so hard to understand sometimes—she didn't want to jump to any conclusions about what he was trying to tell her.

This time he was silent for so long that she was sure he'd decided to drop the whole subject. But finally he spoke again. "You can't have it both ways," he said. "It's not fair. Starlight needs more than that. He deserves it."

The words hit Carole like a sledgehammer. She wasn't sure what to think, how to feel, how to respond. For one thing, she was amazed that Ben was sitting there telling her this. Ben Marlow, the guy who would probably be happy if every other human on the planet were wiped out by some kind of virus and he could be completely alone with his beloved horses. The guy who'd looked at her as if she'd sprouted three heads and tentacles when she'd suggested that they dance together at the party. The guy who was so protective of his own privacy that he'd stopped speaking to her for a while over the summer after she'd dared to follow him home, curious about where he lived.

But now here he was, involving himself in her life. Revealing that he'd been paying a lot more attention than she'd realized.

She would have to think more about that later. Right now, though, she had to figure out how to react to what he'd just said. "S-Starlight is fine," she protested weakly. But his eyes, steady on hers now, revealed that he wasn't buying it. "Really," she added. "Um, I know I've been kind of busy with Samson and other stuff lately."

"Other stuff?" he repeated.

She shrugged sheepishly. "Okay, mostly Samson," she admitted. "But so what? I mean, what does that mean?"

Even before Ben could answer, she suddenly saw the answer to her own question. It flashed in her mind so clearly that she couldn't believe she'd avoided seeing it until then. What it meant was that she loved two wonderful horses, two noble creatures that both deserved a rider who would make them number one, cherish them above all others. She had been concentrating most of her love and attention on Samson lately, glorying in their budding partnership even as she prepared for the big show. She hadn't even noticed that she'd also been neglecting Starlight—emotionally, if not physically. That couldn't go on. Even though she hadn't spent much time with him lately, she still loved him so much. . . .

"You have a choice to make," Ben said. He looked down at the bit he was still holding. After staring at it for a moment, he started polishing it again.

Carole's head was spinning. Samson or Starlight. How could she choose between them? It was impossible. She couldn't imagine her life without either one.

And why should I have to, anyway? she wondered, feeling defiant as she glanced at Ben, who was concentrating on his work. *Who says I have to choose? After the Colesford show I'll have more time to spend with Starlight. As long as Max lets me keep riding Samson, I know I can make time for him, too. There's no reason I can't love them both equally. . . .*

She sighed, wondering if she was being naive. Her life had been awfully busy even before Samson had come to Pine Hollow. And that didn't seem likely to change anytime soon. She had already promised herself that once the horse show was behind her, she would spend more time on her schoolwork. And Max had been asking her to help teach riding classes more often lately. With everything else she had to do . . .

"I don't know," she told Ben in despair. "I just don't know what to think—what to do." She glanced at him hesitantly. "What do you think?"

He shrugged without looking up from his task. "Doesn't matter what I think."

"It matters to me," Carole insisted. "I mean, I don't even know what my choices really are here. What can I do about any of this, anyway?"

This time he glanced up, his face somber. "It's tough," he said with a touch of sympathy in his gruff voice. "I wish I—uh, well. But it's your life. You've got to figure out what you want. Otherwise it'll never work out."

Carole gave him a surprised glance. For Ben, it had been an eloquent speech. Still, she couldn't help feeling a tiny bit annoyed with him. Eloquent or not, his comments weren't very helpful. "Whatever," she said miserably.

He gazed at her. "No, really," he said. Returning his gaze to his work, he cleared his throat. "Believe me, I know—it can tear you up. But, you know, you have to do it."

"What do you mean?" Carole asked cautiously, catching a new note in his voice. A sad, thoughtful, slightly bitter tone she'd never heard before.

Ben shrugged. "Nothing," he mumbled. "I mean—well—nothing."

"Fine." Carole sighed, wondering why she'd thought he might be able to help her with this. She should have known better.

"I was fifteen," Ben said abruptly.

Carole was taken aback. "Huh?"

Ben scowled at her. "You can't—uh, I mean, I don't like to talk about—well."

"I won't tell anyone," Carole promised, guessing what he was driving at.

He shot her a suspicious look, but then nodded. "Okay, well, anyway. My mother had just died. That was—well, tough."

Carole's eyes widened. She had seen where Ben lived—when she had followed him home that day, he'd returned to a tiny, cramped, ramshackle house, where a feeble old man had struggled to retrieve a few pieces of dingy laundry from the line strung across the rocky, weed-infested yard. There had been no signs that anyone else lived there besides the old man and Ben. Carole had often wondered what had happened to his parents, but she'd never worked up the nerve to ask.

I guess we do have something in common besides horses after all, she thought, thinking of her own mother, remembering how devastated she'd been after she had died of cancer all those years ago. How much she still missed her.

"I know," she told Ben quietly. "I've been there."

She wanted to say more, but she stopped herself, afraid that he might clam up again.

"Anyway." He shrugged and tossed the bit, clean and shiny now, into the bucket in the corner of the room. "It wasn't long after that when my old man . . . well, anyway, I found myself needing a new place to live."

Carole crinkled her brow in confusion. Had Ben's father died, too? Something in his expression made her think that wasn't what had happened. She opened her mouth to ask, but he was already speaking again.

"I have an aunt and uncle," Ben said. "In Philadelphia. Both accountants. Nice house, the works. They wanted me to live there." He shrugged. "Even offered money for college."

The last words were spoken quietly, almost as if he were speaking more to himself than to Carole. Once again she felt a twinge of surprise. She knew that Ben's dream was to enroll in an equine studies program. Only a lack of money had stopped him— except now it seemed that the money had been there if he'd wanted it.

"Why didn't you—" she blurted before thinking. Then she gulped. "Um, I mean, I guess there must have been a reason you decided not to live with them."

Ben's expression was pained—Carole could tell it was a struggle for him to carry on this conversation at all. "Yeah," he said. "It was a trade-off. I already knew, well . . ." He waved an arm to indicate the stable around them.

"You knew you wanted to be around horses," Carole said. It was a statement, not a question. Ben had been born to work with horses, just as she had.

He rubbed his cheek, staring off into space. "That wasn't going to happen. Not where they live."

Suddenly it all made sense to Carole. "You mean if you'd gone to live with them, you couldn't have worked with horses. So you came here instead, even though . . ." She let her voice trail off, blushing slightly as she remembered how she had sat in her car that day the summer before, shocked at the poverty of Ben's home.

"Yeah. Besides, my grandfather lets me do my own thing." Ben shrugged. "My aunt and uncle . . . well. Anyway, I didn't really want to stick around so close to . . ." He shook his head and glanced at Carole again. "Doesn't matter. The point is, people tried to tell me what I should do. Thought they knew what was best."

"But they didn't." Carole nodded thoughtfully, pondering what Ben had just revealed about himself. He had given up a life that would have been comfortable, easy, secure—ignored the people who thought they knew what was best for him. He'd made a difficult decision about what was most important in his life. Carole looked at him with new respect. "Wow." Suddenly it dawned on her how unusual this conversation really was. Ben had never before volunteered anything the least bit personal about himself, and now here he was, practically spilling his guts to her. It made her feel much closer to him all of a sudden. "This is great," she blurted out. "I mean, you know, that you're telling me this. Being so open and everything. Uh, wait. I mean—"

Too late, she saw his usual guarded expression return, as if a curtain had fallen over his eyes. She realized she'd said too much, intruded a step too far into his personal space. She gulped, wishing she could take back her words, knowing she'd said the wrong thing to him once again.

"It's late," he said in his usual brusque manner, not meeting her eye as he stood and dropped his rag on the counter by the sink. "I've got to go."

Before Carole could say a word to stop him, he was gone.

SEVEN

The next evening, Callie picked at a loose thread on her skirt as Scott spun the wheel to take the turn into the Willow Creek High School driveway. "I have a bad feeling about this," she muttered darkly.

Scott glanced over at her. "Come on, Callie," he said with a smile. "This is supposed to be fun, remember?"

Callie didn't answer. She just stared with trepidation at the modern glass-and-brick building, light pouring through its windows and casting yellowish patterns on the darkened sidewalk. George didn't have a car, so she had agreed to meet him at the dance. Thanks to a last-minute phone call from Stevie insisting that Scott wear a tie and sport jacket instead of the sweater he'd put on, she was now a few minutes late. She scanned the students gathered in the courtyard in front of the school doors as Scott steered past on his way to the parking lot. She didn't see George, but she was sure he was there. He wasn't the type to be late on an evening like this.

"Okay," Scott said cheerfully as he pulled into a parking space and cut the engine. "Ready to make an entrance?"

"I don't know what you're so happy about," Callie muttered. "Aren't you afraid Veronica's going to dump a bucket of pig's blood on your head or something?"

Scott chuckled. "Come on," he said, opening his door and climbing out.

Callie gathered her crutches and did the same. Outside, she leaned over to give her face one last check in the side-view mirror, then straightened the collar of her silk blouse. "Let's go," she told Scott.

Soon the two of them were walking across the asphalt toward the front of the school. They had almost reached the courtyard when George spotted them and hurried forward to meet them.

"Hi, Callie," he said breathlessly, hardly seeming to notice Scott, who ducked away and headed for the door alone. "Wow, you look incredible."

"Thanks. You look nice, too." She had to admit that it was true. He still wasn't going to be mistaken for a male model or anything, but he did look a lot cuter than usual in his well-cut dark suit and tasteful tie, with his short blond hair tamed into neat waves.

Maybe this won't be a total disaster after all, she thought hopefully.

He extended his arm shyly. "Um, shall we?"

She tucked her hand into his elbow, shifting both crutches to her other hand. He supported her carefully as she walked beside him into the school, hardly having to favor her weak right leg at all.

"I think it's this way," George said, turning and following a group of students Callie didn't know down the hall to the left. She hadn't seen anybody else from Fenton Hall yet, though she was sure there would be plenty of people she knew inside. She clutched George's sleeve and wet her lips, glancing around her as they walked. She'd never been inside Willow Creek High School before, though she'd heard Carole and Lisa talk about it often enough.

The gymnasium doors were propped open, and the sound of upbeat dance music poured out to envelop them as they approached. Just inside the entrance, Callie saw a cluster of students gathered around her brother. More people were already hurrying toward him from the crowded dance floor just beyond.

George had noticed, too. "Looks like your brother's campaigning already."

"That's Scott for you." Callie cleared her throat and glanced around as she and George entered the room, skirting Scott's group and then drifting to a stop. She raised her voice to make herself heard over the music. "Wow, there sure are a lot of people here."

That was an understatement. The gym was packed. People were dancing, helping themselves to refreshments from a long table at the far end of the room, or just standing around talking. A girl from

Callie's English class walked past and waved, casting a curious glance at George. Callie waved back, ignoring the glance, though she did remove her hand from his arm, feeling self-conscious.

Then she turned to look at George. He was only about half an inch taller than she was, so she could look him straight in the face. "So . . . ," she said, not sure what they were supposed to do next.

He didn't seem to know, either. "So," he replied. "Um, would you like something to drink?" He waved a hand toward the refreshments.

"Sure. That would be great." Callie smiled at him thankfully, realizing that her throat was a little dry.

She followed as he made his way through the crowds, wielding her crutches expertly and nodding at people she knew as she went. Soon they reached the refreshment table, and George poured her a cup of soda. She sipped at it and glanced around, wondering why she suddenly couldn't think of a single intelligent thing to say. She and George had talked together often enough before this, usually about chemistry or riding. But somehow, neither of those subjects seemed appropriate at this point, though no alternative topics presented themselves to Callie's mind.

George seemed to be having similar problems. He cleared his throat several times, coughed into his hand, and then smiled brightly at her over the rim of his paper cup. "Well," he said after a long moment of silence. "This is nice, isn't it?"

"Sure." Callie wasn't certain what he was referring to, but it didn't seem to matter. "Everyone seems to be having fun."

At that moment, several large guys raced to the deejay's table, where one of them grabbed the microphone. "Willow Creek *rules*!" he bellowed, while his friends whooped and pumped their fists in the air. Laughter and cheers erupted from the dancing students, and several people echoed the large guy's words as the deejay wrestled the microphone back.

"I guess that means they won their game today," Callie commented with a smile, suddenly remembering that this was Willow Creek High School's homecoming, not just a normal dance.

"What?" George said, glancing toward the commotion. "Oh, uh, I guess." He shrugged. "I don't know, I'm not really into sports."

"Oh." Callie wasn't sure what to say to that. She took another sip of soda, feeling uncomfortable. Just then another song started. "Hey, I like this one," she said, her foot tapping along automatically.

"Would you like to dance?" George asked.

"Sure." Callie smiled with relief. Of course. They were at a dance—why not start dancing? She already knew from Stevie's party that George was a good dancer, even though he didn't look as if he should be. Leaning her crutches against the table, she took the hand he offered and limped onto the dance floor after him.

For a while, she did her best simply to enjoy herself. And for a while, it almost worked. George's physical awkwardness seemed to melt away when he danced, much as it did when he was in the saddle.

Still, Callie wasn't kidding herself. She had known almost from the moment she'd arrived at the dance that things were never going to work out between her and George. She liked him just fine as a friend, but she was never going to be able to see him as a boyfriend. No way. It just wasn't going to happen. She already suspected that just surviving this dance was going to take all the endurance she had.

"Having fun?" George asked, interrupting her thoughts. His eyes were slightly anxious as he looked at her, and Callie realized she must have been frowning as she tried to figure things out.

She forced a pleasant smile, tossing her long blond hair off her face. "Of course," she told him. "Are you?"

"Definitely." George's voice was fervent. He pulled her a little closer as they danced, even though an up-tempo song was playing, and she did her best not to pull away again.

This isn't going to be easy, she thought as she felt his hand gently rubbing the small of her back. *I've got to find a way to tell him this isn't working. No, it won't be easy at all.*

At that moment Stevie was on her hands and knees on the kitchen floor, scrubbing at a stubborn grease spot. She wiped her brow and glanced at her twin, who was across the room balancing precariously on a chair as he carefully unscrewed a dusty glass shade from the overhead light fixture. Their parents had left an hour earlier to take the twins' younger brother, Michael, to dinner and a movie in town. The only one home keeping Stevie and Alex company was the family dog, a big, lazy golden retriever named Bear. And all he seemed interested in doing was licking the floor as Stevie washed it.

"Get away," she told the dog grumpily, shoving at him as he lowered his nose to the spot she was attacking. "This sucks enough without having to deal with dog slobber, too."

Bear gave her a quizzical look, then stretched toward her and slurped at her face.

"Eeeew!" she exclaimed, squeezing her eyes shut and throwing her sponge at the dog. "Come on, Bear! Quit it!"

"Quit it yourself, Stevie," Alex said sharply. He had climbed down from the chair and was dunking the dusty shade into a bucket of soapy water. "It's not the dog's fault we're stuck here making like Mr. Clean while all our friends are at the dance."

Stevie shot her brother a disgruntled look, sitting back on her heels to rest her back. "I know," she snapped back. "It's *your* fault. If you hadn't had the bright idea to start guzzling beer last weekend—"

"Hey, I wasn't the only one guzzling," Alex reminded her with a frown.

Stevie rolled her eyes, wishing her parents had assigned her and Alex jobs in different rooms. He'd been whining all day about not getting to go to the dance with Lisa. *As if he's the only one missing out,* she thought. She had made Scott promise to call her from the dance a few times if he could to keep her updated. But he hadn't called yet, even though the dance had started nearly an hour earlier, and Stevie was driving herself crazy wondering what evil plans Veronica might be putting into action while she sat there scraping caked-on grease off the linoleum.

"Whatever," she muttered in Alex's general direction, rolling her shoulders back and forth to loosen the knots in her tired muscles.

Alex wiped halfheartedly at the soapy shade with a rag. "Lisa and I were really looking forward to this dance," he murmured sadly. "It would have been so great. . . ."

Before Stevie could respond, the phone rang. She jumped, her heart flipping over with an uneasy combination of relief and anxiety. "That must be Scott!" she exclaimed, dashing for the phone and dodging around Bear as he nudged at her abandoned sponge with his nose. She grabbed the receiver in the middle of the second ring. "Hello?" she barked breathlessly. "Scott?"

"Not," a familiar voice responded. "Sorry to disappoint."

"Oh. Phil." Stevie slumped against the wall and let out a long breath. "Hi. I thought you were going to be Scott."

"Obviously." Phil sounded slightly miffed. "I guess you'll just have to settle for me. Too bad."

Stevie frowned. What was he sounding so worked up about? Whatever it was, she didn't have the energy to deal with it at the moment. She had too many other things to worry about. "What do you want?" she asked shortly. "I'm kind of in the middle of something here."

"I thought your parents weren't going to be home," Phil said. "I figured that meant we'd have time to talk. We've hardly talked all week, in case you didn't notice."

"There are a few reasons for that, remember?" she retorted. "Number one of which is, I'm grounded for the next million years or so, and Mom and Dad are working my fingers to the bone on top of it."

"Hmmph." Phil didn't sound particularly sympathetic. "Well, that hasn't stopped you from putting in your time getting ready for the horse show. Not to mention holding Scott's hand through his little campaign."

"Don't be an idiot. You know how important that stuff is." Stevie noticed Alex raising an eyebrow at her as he listened, and she turned her back to him, facing the wall. "I mean, people are counting on me."

"Right," Phil said with a definite edge to his voice. "Well, just so we both know what your priorities are."

Stevie was really getting fed up with his griping.

Had he called just to make her feel even worse than she already did? Did he think she enjoyed having to squeeze in everything she had to do between joyous activities like wiping sticky cobwebs out of the attic beams and scraping old wallpaper off the bathroom walls? If so, maybe it was time for him to get a clue.

"Look, Mom and Dad will be home soon," she said curtly. "If the stupid kitchen isn't spotless by the time they get here, they'll probably chain me in the basement or something. So I'd better go."

"Whatever," Phil said. "Sorry to bother you. Later."

"Later," she replied before slamming down the phone.

An hour later, from her seat beside George on the bottom row of bleachers, Callie caught a glimpse of her brother heading for the dance floor with yet another pretty girl in tow. She shook her head, wondering if he planned to dance with every girl in the place before the night was over. She hadn't been paying particularly close attention to him, but as usual he had been hard to miss completely. He always had that effect—wherever he went, people noticed him. Their father was the same way. Not for the first time, Callie wished that some of their effortless social skills would rub off on her. She didn't care about being the center of attention—far from it—but it would be nice to always know the right thing to say to people. People like George, for instance . . .

She smiled blandly as he continued talking about the Colesford Horse Show. She had brought up the topic as soon as they'd stopped dancing, figuring it would put them back on safe, friendly ground. But she was finding it difficult to concentrate on what he was saying.

Taking a sip of the punch George had fetched for her, she let her gaze wander over the rest of the room. She knew she should be making more of an effort to talk to him, but it was taking all of her acting skills just to pretend she was having a tolerable time. In truth, she was keeping a close eye on the clock above the basketball net on the far side of the gym, willing its hands to move faster. She had already realized that the downside of riding to the dance with Scott was that she would have to wait until he was ready to leave, and she knew that probably wouldn't be until the bitter end.

At that moment her gaze wandered to a spot just beyond the dance floor. Veronica diAngelo was standing there. A good-looking guy was talking to her, but she clearly wasn't listening. Her gaze was trained on Scott, and Callie was surprised he couldn't feel her eyes burning into his back.

Wow, Callie thought, taking another sip of punch. *If looks could kill, Scott would be a cinder right now.*

But she didn't waste much time thinking about that. Veronica had been shooting Scott dirty looks all evening, and so far it didn't seem to be bothering him one bit.

At that moment George put a hand on her arm. She jumped, startled at the contact. "Anyway," he said, "I hope you're planning to come and cheer us on at the show."

She raised her punch cup to her lips again, using it as an excuse to dislodge his hand. "Sure," she said after swallowing. "Of course I am."

"Good." George looked pleased. "Um, I'm sure it will make me ride better. Just knowing you're watching, I mean."

Callie didn't know what to say, so she just smiled again. *This is awful,* she thought, feeling terribly guilty. *The poor guy is trying so hard, and he doesn't even realize how totally it's not working.*

She didn't think he'd even noticed that she'd been tuning out most of what he said, hardly listening as he talked about school, his mother, his horse . . . She certainly hoped he didn't realize that every word he said was turning her off more and more.

"I'm having a really nice time with you tonight, Callie," he said. He gazed at her earnestly. "I never thought a girl like you—well, I mean, I'm feeling like the luckiest guy here right now because I'm sitting with you."

"I'm having a nice time, too," she lied, wanting to spare his feelings as much as possible. After all, it wasn't really his fault that this wasn't working out. She was sure there were plenty of girls out there who would appreciate him for the sweet, wonderful, caring guy he was, but unfortunately she just wasn't one of them.

How could I ever have thought this would work? she wondered desperately, sneaking another glance at the clock as George tipped his head back and gulped down the last few drops of his punch.

Just then she noticed Betsy Cavanaugh and Nicole Adams standing nearby giggling to each other with their heads close together. Callie narrowed her eyes as Nicole glanced straight at her and then turned away quickly, nudging Betsy and giggling more than ever.

What's up with them? Callie wondered. She barely knew either girl—they were in a few of her classes, but they'd never shown any signs of noticing her before.

"This punch is good, isn't it?" George set his empty cup carefully on the seat beside him.

"It's okay. Maybe a little too sweet." Out of the corner of her eye, Callie saw that Betsy and Nicole were peeking at her again. Since she figured George would have let her know if she'd smudged her lipstick across her face or had something hanging out of her nose, she could only assume that they were marveling at what an odd couple the two of them made.

Callie did her best not to think about that. Growing up in a well-known family, she'd long since become accustomed to getting more than her share of attention. She'd never liked it much, but she'd learned to ignore it.

"I thought you liked sweet things," George said, clearly oblivious to the extra attention they were attracting. "I've seen you eating those brownies Max's wife makes sometimes."

Callie shot him a quick glance, wondering just how much he'd noticed about her without her realizing it. "That's different," she said, trying to keep her voice light and casual. "I'll eat anything chocolate."

"Really?" George looked interested. He leaned a little closer. "Is that your favorite food?"

"I guess so."

Betsy and Nicole had moved out of sight, but Callie had just spotted Valerie Watkins, Scott's main competitor, standing near the refreshment table with several friends. They were all staring at Scott, which wasn't particularly strange. But then Valerie pushed her glasses up on her nose and turned her head from side to side, obviously searching for someone in the crowds. Finally her gaze landed on Callie. When she saw Callie staring back at her, she blinked and turned away quickly, grabbing the nearest friend and whispering something. The friend cast Callie a brief glance, then turned away, covering her face to hide a smile.

Callie frowned. Didn't the people at this dance have anything better to do than laugh at her date? She was getting fed up with it. The worst part was that she knew that if she had actually been interested

110

in George, other people's reactions wouldn't have bothered her at all. She wouldn't even have noticed them. But as it was, she felt herself cringing at their watchful eyes, their laughter and whispers. She hated herself for it, but she couldn't help the way she felt.

At that moment the deejay switched to a slow, dreamy song, and Callie bit back a groan as George turned to her. "Had enough rest yet?" he asked hopefully.

"Um . . ." The last thing she felt like doing was slow-dancing with George, but what could she say?

"Uh, hey, Callie." A new voice interrupted her thoughts. Glancing up, she saw a tall, broad-shouldered guy with longish brown hair standing in front of her.

She vaguely recognized him from her Latin class—she was pretty sure they'd been in the same discussion group a couple of weeks earlier. She searched her memory for his name. *Kenny,* she remembered. *Kenny Lamb.*

"Hey, Kenny," she greeted him brightly, relieved at the timely interruption. "How's it going?"

Kenny glanced uncertainly at George, who had already started to climb to his feet and was caught in an awkward half-standing position. He was looking up at Kenny with wide, startled eyes. "Look, I don't want to interrupt anything or whatever," Kenny said, turning back to Callie. "But I was just wondering if, well, if you'd like to dance."

"Sure," Callie said quickly. She tried not to notice

George's crestfallen expression as she stood, wavering slightly on her bad leg. She felt guilty about accepting the other guy's offer, especially when George had already all but asked her himself, but the strain of pretending she was having fun was really getting to her. She needed a break. "As long as you don't mind holding me up a little." She gestured at her crutches, still leaning against the bleachers.

"No problem at all." Kenny grinned and held out his arm.

Callie gave George a quick smile. "See you in a minute, okay?" she said, doing her best to avoid his forlorn gaze.

"Um, okay," he said softly. "I'll be right here."

Callie felt her heart twist with pity. But all she could think of was getting away from him for a little while, taking a few deep breaths, and figuring out what to do. Without another backward glance, she took Kenny's arm and limped toward the dance floor at his side, feeling as if she'd just escaped from prison.

EIGHT

Lisa was feeling at loose ends. She stretched and yawned, glancing up from her calculus homework to check the time on the digital clock by her bed. It was almost nine-thirty, which meant that Rafe would probably be turning up at any moment—her mother had mentioned that he was coming over after his shift at the store. Lisa grimaced at the thought. Under most circumstances she would have been thrilled that her mother was finally seeing somebody. Mrs. Atwood had been bitter and depressed ever since her divorce from Lisa's father, and Lisa knew it was doing her mother a lot of good to get out and have fun again.

But why did she have to choose Rafe? Lisa wondered. She had disliked her mother's new boyfriend from the moment she met him, and not only because he was a good twenty years younger than Mrs. Atwood. His lazy, laid-back attitude really rubbed her the wrong way. Of course, it also hadn't helped that she'd had no idea of his existence until the day she'd walked in on him groping her mother in the living room.

Lisa shook her head and pushed back her chair. She couldn't stay there with Rafe coming over. She wasn't in the mood to be polite to him tonight.

She walked briskly toward her bedroom door, then stopped, wondering where exactly she could go. *If only Alex weren't grounded,* she thought, *we'd be at the dance right now, having fun.*

Still, she had no interest in going to the dance without her boyfriend, no matter how desperate she was to get out. Visiting Alex and Stevie was out, too, of course—their parents were being pretty strict about visitors.

Her gaze wandered to the top shelf of her bookcase, where the riding trophies and ribbons she'd won over the years were displayed. She smiled, suddenly realizing the answer to her problem was right there in front of her.

Of course, she thought. *I'll go to Pine Hollow. I haven't checked on Prancer in a couple of days.*

She knew it was a little late by stable standards—the horses would have been fed their evening meal, and Max was probably up at his house on the hill beyond the stable, helping his wife put their two daughters to bed. Red and Denise would have departed as well, driving off in Denise's battered pickup to the apartment they shared in town.

But I'd bet a cookie that Carole's still there, Lisa thought, giving her reflection a quick check in the mirror over her dresser before heading for the door once again. *She's been spending all her time there getting ready for the horse show. It will be good for the two of us to hang out for a while. Make sure things are back to normal between us after what happened last weekend.*

Lisa had been furious with Carole when she'd learned that Carole had told Alex about what Skye had said. But she had quickly realized that it had been an accident. The two of them had made up the day after the party, but Lisa hadn't forgotten the incident, and she was sure Carole hadn't either. It couldn't hurt to spend a little time together and finish working things out.

Hurrying down the stairs, Lisa glanced around for her mother. But Mrs. Atwood was nowhere to be seen, and Lisa soon deduced that she was in the shower getting ready for her date. Lisa couldn't help feeling relieved. She would be able to escape without taking a chance of getting sucked into a conversation about all Rafe's wonderful qualities, which was the only thing her mother seemed to talk about these days. After scribbling a note explaining where she was going, Lisa went to the refrigerator and dug out the plastic freezer bag of carrot pieces that she'd prepared for the next time she saw Prancer. Then she slipped on her jacket, dropped the bag in her pocket, and headed outside, deciding to walk instead of drive. Pine Hollow was only ten minutes' walk through the fields, it was a warm night for early November, and she wasn't in a hurry.

When she reached the stable grounds and crossed the gravel parking lot, Lisa saw that her guess had been right. The only car parked there was Carole's dingy, sagging red-and-rust sedan.

Lisa let herself into the stable. The bright overheads were still on, and she could hear the sound of hoofbeats from the propped-open doorway of the indoor ring. Peeking inside, Lisa saw that Carole was riding Samson over a jump course in the center of the ring, her face intense with concentration. Lisa stood and watched them for a moment, admiring the fluid movements and almost effortless jumping action of the big black gelding. It was hard to believe sometimes that this was the same Samson she and her friends had helped bring into the world, the same feisty little colt that had struggled to stand on his long, spindly legs, almost tipping over when his dam turned to nose at him gently. . . .

Thinking about foals reminded her of Prancer. Slipping away to give Carole time to finish her workout, Lisa turned down the aisle leading to the mare's stall.

Prancer was dozing in the corner of her stall when Lisa poked her head over the door, but she awoke with a start and came forward eagerly when Lisa unlatched the door to let herself inside.

"Hey, sweetie," Lisa greeted the horse fondly. She rubbed her neck and scratched her under her mane.

"Looks like I caught you napping. Feel like going for a walk?"

Earlier that week, Max had suggested that Lisa help him out by leading Prancer slowly around the stable several times a week to let her stretch her legs, since she was confined to her stall or Pine Hollow's smallest paddock most of the time because of her risky pregnancy. He had made the suggestion casually, implying that he had only thought of Lisa for the job because she was the one who'd ridden Prancer the most over the last few years. Lisa had agreed, holding back her knowing smile until Max had moved on. She didn't want him to catch on that Carole had let her in on a wonderful, amazing secret—that Mr. Atwood was in the process of arranging to buy the mare from Pine Hollow as a surprise graduation gift for Lisa. Graduation wasn't until June, the same month that Prancer's foals were due. Sometimes Lisa wondered if she would be able to carry on that long without giving herself away. Every time she looked at the beautiful, gentle, sweet-natured Thoroughbred she'd grown to love so much over the years—the only horse she could imagine owning—she felt alternating thrills of joy and nervousness. After all, they still had to get through this pregnancy, and a lot of things could happen when twins were involved.

Clipping a lead rope to the mare's halter, Lisa led her out of the stall. Prancer placed her long legs carefully as she crossed the threshold, snorting softly and keeping her head close to Lisa's shoulder.

"I know," Lisa said. "It feels good to get out of that stall for a while, right?"

She led Prancer down the long aisle toward the back exit. On her way over, Lisa had decided that it was more than warm enough to take Prancer outdoors for her exercise. The fresh air would do them both good. Soon the two of them were walking down the hard-packed path leading past the back paddock and a couple of outbuildings before curving around to return to the stable.

As they walked, Lisa's mind wandered forward to the wonderful day when Prancer's foals—she was being optimistic and thinking in the plural, though she was aware that there was a good chance both babies wouldn't survive—were weaned and the mare was all Lisa's. Still, Lisa was sensible enough to realize that she had some important decisions to make before that day ever arrived.

She sighed, wondering if it had even occurred to her father that owning a horse could have a real impact on her college plans. Lisa had long since come up with a list of eight schools she planned to apply to, and she had already sent off her applications for four of them—two in Virginia and two in Southern California. Keeping Prancer nearby wouldn't be a problem at any of the four. The Virginia schools were both less than two hours' drive from Willow Creek—NVU, the school that had already accepted her, was only forty miles away—which meant that she would be able to continue to board Prancer at Pine Hollow and ride her on weekends. The other two schools were close to where her father lived, which meant not only that he could help her find a stable where she could board her, but also that there would be someone to check on the mare during Lisa's visits back East.

"But what about the next two schools on my list?" Lisa murmured to Prancer, reaching up to scratch her under the chin. "I mean, one of them's in the middle of Boston, and the other one's in Chicago. Where would I keep you then? Who would help me take care of you, make sure you were getting enough exercise?"

Prancer didn't answer, of course, and Lisa sighed, knowing it was up to her to come up with a course of action. The problem wasn't going to go away, and she'd be better off facing that now and adjusting her plans accordingly. If owning Prancer was going to mean that she couldn't go to those far-flung schools, it would be better if she didn't even waste her time applying.

Of course, to be honest with herself, Lisa had to admit that Prancer was only one of the reasons she was worried about some of the colleges on her list. She had chosen them in her usual thoughtful, rational way, deciding that they offered courses that interested her and had excellent academic reputations as well as diverse social opportunities and extra-curricular activities.

But now that she was faced with the idea of actually *going* to them—of flying off to some strange city, where she wouldn't know a soul, miles and miles from her family and friends—she was having serious doubts. How would her relationship with Alex survive another separation? He would still have another year of high school to go, so that would mean a minimum of a year apart. It had been hard enough for him to deal with her being gone for a couple of months the previous summer—she wasn't sure how he would handle a longer separation, no matter how many academic advantages those faraway schools offered.

Alex wasn't the only one she would be leaving behind, either. Her mother had been a lot more self-sufficient since she'd started dating Rafe, but Lisa was afraid that when the relationship crashed—and she was sure it would, probably sooner rather than later—Mrs. Atwood would slide back into the gloomy, helpless mood that had consumed her before. Would she see Lisa's departure as yet another betrayal?

Then there were Lisa's friends, of course. She knew that Carole and Stevie would stand by her decision, no matter what it was. But it would be hard to be so far from her best friends, especially since they, like Alex, would still be in high school.

"It doesn't really seem worth it when you get right

down to it, does it, girl?" Lisa mused aloud, pausing on the path to allow Prancer to stretch her nose curiously toward a branch of the gnarled old apple tree near the paddock. "I mean, to go through all that and not even be near Dad, like I would be at the colleges in California . . ." She didn't bother to carry the thought any further, realizing that while there were a few big advantages to the schools in California, her boyfriend and her mother would probably have even more of a problem with her going there than they would with the schools in Chicago and Boston.

She sighed with frustration, staring off into space as Prancer lowered her head to nibble at a patch of grass near the apple tree. No matter how many times she listed the pros and cons of every possible decision, she still didn't know what to do. Those faraway schools offered plenty of academic challenges. But was that enough to make up for what she would be leaving behind? She wished she believed in fortune-tellers. This year would be a whole lot easier if she had some kind of idea what her future would bring.

"What do you think, Prancer?" Lisa asked. "Which school do you think is the best one for me—or rather, for *us*?"

Prancer nudged at her shoulder, bored with the grass, and Lisa suddenly remembered the bag full of carrot pieces in her pocket. Fishing it out, she offered the mare several of the carrots on her open palm.

"There you go," she said as Prancer quickly slurped up the snack, then looked at her, waiting for more. Max and the vet had okayed treats for the pregnant mare as long as she didn't overdo it, so Lisa had carefully rationed out a small portion. She shook the rest of the carrot pieces out of the bag.

It didn't take long for Prancer to finish off the treats. She snorted and shoved at Lisa's chest, clearly looking for yet another helping.

"Sorry," Lisa said, giving Prancer a pat. "That's it for today, okay?"

Prancer didn't seem satisfied with that. She nosed curiously at Lisa's jacket pocket and a moment later came up with something clutched firmly in her big teeth.

"Hey," Lisa protested with a laugh. "What are you doing, you big goofball? That's not edible. It's just . . ." She paused, not sure what it was that Prancer had grabbed except that it was some kind of folded paper. "That better not be my computer science problem sheet," she warned jokingly, yanking the papers away from the mare and wiping them on her jeans. "I don't think my teacher would believe me if I told him that a horse ate my . . ."

Her voice trailed off as she looked at the paper and realized what it was. It was her acceptance letter to Northern Virginia University. Until that moment, she'd completely forgotten shoving it into her jacket pocket the day before.

Lisa stared at the letter for a long moment before

turning to gaze at Prancer, who had given up on treats and was nibbling at the grass again. "Wow," Lisa muttered. "That's weird. If I didn't know better, I'd think you just answered my question about where I should go to school next year."

She blinked. She had meant the comment jokingly. But suddenly she wondered if she wasn't missing something here. Maybe Prancer had grabbed the letter randomly, but that didn't mean that Lisa couldn't take it as a sign—a little nudge from the cosmos, a hint about what she should do.

NVU, she thought, feeling her heart start to beat a little faster. *They've already accepted me into their honors program. They even offered me a scholarship. It's a good college, with most of the courses I want, and it's close to home. What more am I looking for? Am I making things too difficult for myself by worrying so much about those other schools?*

She stared at Prancer, her mind suddenly flooded with images of how easy it could be. All she had to do was follow this omen and make the decision to go to NVU, and everything else would fall into place. Her future with Prancer would be assured, since the mare could remain at Pine Hollow. Alex would be so thrilled that she would be close to home next year that he probably wouldn't even remember to be upset about her Thanksgiving trip to California. Her mother would feel better having her relatively close to home. Both her parents would have an easier time paying her tuition, since NVU was one of the least expensive schools on her list and she'd been awarded scholarship money. Lisa could still spend plenty of time with her friends. She even knew a few people who already attended NVU—Stevie's older brother, Chad; a couple of old friends from riding camp; some acquaintances from school—and she probably wouldn't be the only Willow Creek High student from her class to enroll there in the fall, so she would start off knowing people instead of having to start all over again trying to make new friends. In general, she wouldn't have to worry anymore about any of the problems that had been nagging at her lately— she'd be free to enjoy her senior year of high school.

"Maybe I've been making this way more difficult than it needs to be," she said wonderingly, stroking Prancer's shoulder absently as the mare continued to graze. She took a deep breath and smiled as a wild, powerful impulse grabbed her. Why shouldn't she do it? Why shouldn't she go with her gut for a change? Something was telling her it was the right thing to do. "I'll do it. I'll mail in my response on Monday," she told the mare briskly. "Then everything will be settled, and I can relax."

That sounded like the best news she'd heard in months. Suddenly she was so excited about her decision that she wasn't sure she'd be able to wait until Monday. Still clutching the acceptance letter in one hand, she tugged on Prancer's lead, eager to get back to the stable. Carole would still be there, and Lisa

124

was glad—she couldn't wait to share her big news with someone.

Carole checked Samson's water bucket and then gave the big black gelding a pat. "There you go, boy," she said. "All settled in for the night. See you tomorrow."

Samson snorted softly and nudged at her, almost as if he were pushing her toward the stall door. Carole laughed.

"Okay, okay," she said. "I know you need your beauty sleep. I'm going."

She was latching the stall door from the outside, her eyes still trained on Samson as he moved around his stall, when she heard someone calling her name. Turning, she saw Lisa hurrying toward her, her cheeks flushed and her eyes gleaming.

"Hi," Carole greeted her, realizing she hadn't seen her friend in days. "You look excited. Prancer didn't decide to have her foals eight months early, did she?"

"Nope. But I do have something I'm dying to tell someone."

Carole hoisted Samson's saddle off the edge of the stall where she'd set it and slung his bridle over her shoulder. "Come on, then," she said. "I've got some tack to clean, and that always goes faster when there's someone there entertaining me while I work."

Lisa nodded and fell into step beside Carole as they headed down the aisle. "Another thrilling Saturday night, huh?" she said cheerfully. "Forget parties and stuff—cleaning tack is what it's all about."

Carole smiled, though she wasn't sure she quite understood why cleaning tack was any funnier just because it was Saturday. She knew that Lisa usually spent Saturday evening on a date with Alex or out with a larger group of friends. But Carole had never really seen what the big deal was about that one particular night. Horses still needed to be fed and exercised and groomed on Saturday, just like any other night of the week.

"So what's your big announcement?" she asked as she and Lisa crossed the stable entryway and entered the narrow hall leading to the tack room.

"I've decided where I'm going to college next year."

"Really?" Carole felt an all-too-familiar flash of startled confusion—the kind she always got when she had totally lost track of time. But then she frowned, realizing that this time she wasn't really that far off schedule. "Wait a minute," she protested. "It's only October."

"November," Lisa corrected with a smile.

"Oops." Carole smiled back. "I mean November." They had reached the tack room, and she led the way inside and dumped her saddle on a handy saddle rack. "I thought you didn't have to make your decision until, like, May or something like that."

"That's true," Lisa said. "But the thing is, I already heard from one of the schools I applied to—NVU. They accepted me into their honors program and offered me a scholarship." She shrugged. "So I've decided to go there."

"NVU?" Carole said. "That's great! You'll be close enough to come home and visit Alex and Stevie and me a lot, and—oh!" she gasped, suddenly realizing another big advantage of Lisa's decision. "You'll be able to keep Prancer at Pine Hollow."

Lisa smiled. "Right. That was one of the things that made me decide to go there. It will make things a whole lot easier if I don't have to worry about her, you know?"

"Sure." Carole was happy that Lisa would stay close the next year, but she couldn't help feeling surprised as well—surprised and a touch uneasy. It wasn't like Lisa to look for the easy answers, and she had been talking for almost a year now about how important it was to her to make a careful choice when it came to deciding where she would go to college. So wasn't this decision a bit impulsive?

I don't really know that it is, Carole reminded herself, hiding her perplexed expression from her friend by leaning over to fish a sponge out of a bucket near the door. *Lisa and I haven't spent that much time together lately. For all I know, she could have been mulling this over for the past month.*

"I'm pretty psyched about it." Lisa reached past Carole to grab a sponge and set to work on Samson's saddle. It was an old habit, automatically helping each other whenever they saw the opportunity, but that didn't stop Carole from shooting her friend a grateful smile as she tackled Samson's bridle.

"I'm really happy for you," Carole said sincerely. "That's a big decision. It's nice that you got it out of the way early."

Still, it wasn't what she would have expected from Lisa. An image of Ben telling her about his past flashed through her mind, and Carole realized that quite a few people hadn't been acting like themselves these days. In fact, she was discovering more and more that people weren't always as predictable as she used to think they were. Sometimes it was simply impossible to guess what was going on inside their heads.

But if that whole mess at the party last week taught me anything, she thought ruefully, *it's that sometimes being a good friend means just being supportive and keeping my mouth shut. Besides, I shouldn't complain—this means Lisa won't be going off to California or someplace next year. I'll still get to see her all the time right here at Pine Hollow.*

"Thanks," Lisa said. "So what's new with you?"

Carole hesitated, her mind jumping once again to Ben. This time she was thinking about the topic that had started their conversation. "Well, I've mostly just been getting ready for the Colesford show," she said. "But I had kind of a weird chat with Ben yesterday."

Lisa raised one eyebrow curiously. "Oh?"

"It was about Samson," Carole said hastily, not wanting Lisa to jump to any wrong conclusions. She knew her friends got some crazy ideas in their heads sometimes about her friendship with Ben. "And—and Starlight."

"What about them?" Lisa suddenly looked a lot less curious, turning her attention to a stubborn bit of dried mud on the saddle flap.

"I guess he's been noticing how much time I've been spending with Samson lately," Carole said slowly. "Um, he was worried about that."

"Why?" Lisa glanced up again, her brow slightly furrowed. "I mean, Max asked you to ride Samson in the show, right? So naturally you're going to spend a lot of time with him. Duh."

Carole bit her lip. "I know," she said. "But it's not just getting ready for the show. Actually I—I think Ben might have noticed something that I wasn't even noticing myself, not until he pointed it out."

"What do you mean?"

"I think . . ." Carole paused and took a deep breath, not sure she was ready to say the words aloud. "I think I may already be more involved with Samson than I realized. And after talking with Ben, I'm starting to wonder if that's fair to Starlight. I—I think I have to decide between them. Soon."

Lisa gasped, dropping her sponge on the saddle and staring at Carole. "What?" she said. "I think I may be losing it. Because I would have sworn I just heard you say you're considering giving up Starlight."

"Not necessarily." Carole gulped, feeling her stomach churn at the very idea of saying good-bye to her beloved horse. "I mean, well, maybe. I guess."

Lisa didn't speak for a moment. "Wow," she said at last. "I always knew you were crazy about Samson, but, well . . ."

"He's an amazing horse," Carole said quietly. She had given up all pretense of cleaning her bridle and simply gazed at Lisa. "We could really learn a lot from each other. Of course, Starlight's pretty great, too."

Lisa's eyes were sympathetic. "I won't say I'm not surprised," she said. "But I guess this is one of those times when you just have to trust what your heart is telling you."

"But what if my heart's telling me two things at the same time?" Carole asked plaintively. "What if it's telling me I love Starlight *and* Samson, and it just won't listen when my head tries to tell it I don't have enough time to give them both the attention they deserve?"

"I don't know." Lisa looked thoughtful. "The only thing I can tell you is that sometimes you really have to pay attention before you can figure out the most honest thing that you feel. It's like when my parents were getting divorced. Remember? I was totally miserable—totally hating life."

Carole nodded. She remembered vividly how unhappy Lisa had been in those days. She had seemed almost like a different person—distracted, irritable, irresponsible, ready to burst into tears at the drop of a hat.

"Well," Lisa went on, "the main thing that helped me get over that was falling in love with Alex. It was like a tiny, sane voice calling to me through the craziness. Once I started listening to it, it kept getting louder, and it kept getting easier for me to go back to being myself."

"Um, okay," Carole said uncertainly, not really sure how that applied to her own situation.

Lisa seemed to realize that she wasn't being clear enough. "I know in my heart that Alex is the guy for me," she explained. "It's the truest thing I know. That's why I could set aside the bad feelings after the divorce and move on, fall in love with him." She shrugged. "It's the same way I feel about Prancer, I guess. She's the most wonderful, special horse I've ever known, and it's not because she's a Thoroughbred or because she's so pretty or anything like that, things I used to think were important, but now I know better. It's just because she's *her*. It's not a logical thing, but it's still true. That's one of the reasons I'm sure my decision about college is the right one."

Carole nodded slowly, thinking about that. *I guess a lot of decisions are harder and more complicated than they look to people from the outside,* she thought. *I would probably never be able to understand all the considerations Lisa took into account when she was try-ing to figure out what to do about college. Just like I could probably never really explain why it's so impor-tant for me to figure out what to do about Samson and Starlight.*

"You just have to look into your heart," Lisa said quietly after a moment. "Sometimes that's the only place you can find the truth."

"Thanks," Carole said. "I guess you're right about that."

She realized belatedly that Ben had been trying to tell her something like that the evening before. He'd been a lot less comfortable expressing it than Lisa was, but in his own way he'd pointed out that the logical choice wasn't necessarily the right one. *Be-cause the logical choice would have been for him to live in Philadelphia with his aunt and uncle,* Carole thought. *But he followed his heart and his true calling instead, even though he knew his life might not be as easy or safe.*

"I see what you mean," she said. "Being logical or doing the easy thing can seem safer, but it can't take the place of figuring out how you really feel."

"Exactly." Lisa smiled sympathetically. "So what's your heart telling you to do?"

"I'm not sure." Carole shook her head. Her thoughts were so jumbled that she was starting to wonder if she would ever be able to untangle them. "I need to think about it some more, I guess. Try to figure things out."

Lisa nodded. "If you want to be alone, I could finish up here," she offered.

"Really?" Carole shot her a grateful look. "Do you mean it?"

"Of course." Lisa waved a hand at her. "What are friends for? Go on."

Carole simply nodded her thanks, suddenly not trusting her voice. Without another word, she hurried out of the tack room and headed toward Samson's stall.

NINE

Callie leaned over the row of sinks in the girls' bathroom and peered into the mirror. She uncapped her tinted lip gloss and ran it over her lips, smacking them together and then grinning widely to make sure she hadn't accidentally turned her teeth Spicy Plum. She hadn't, and she blinked at her own reflection, wondering how much longer she could stay in the bathroom before George started to get suspicious.

She immediately felt guilty about the thought, but she couldn't help it. George had been glued to her side ever since she'd finished her slow dance with Kenny Lamb half an hour earlier, and his attention was becoming almost painful. He seemed pathetically eager to prove to everyone—perhaps most of all to Callie—that they were on a special romantic date.

I only wish I could believe it, Callie thought, still gazing fixedly at herself in the mirror. *I wish I could return his interest. But it's just not happening for me. And I have to figure out what to do about it.*

She jumped slightly as the bathroom door swung

open, then quickly turned away from the mirror and recapped her lip gloss. Glancing at the door, she saw that Lorraine Olsen had entered. Lorraine rode occasionally at Pine Hollow, and she and Callie were in the same history class.

"Hi," Callie said.

"Oh!" Lorraine smiled uncertainly. "Um, hey, Callie. How's it going?"

"Okay." Callie smiled at Lorraine, glad for any distraction from her endlessly circling thoughts about George—and any excuse to postpone going back to the dance, where he was waiting for her. "Are you having fun?"

"Sure." Lorraine pulled a brush out of the small handbag she was carrying and set to work on her hair. "I never realized how many cute guys go to Willow Creek High." She giggled and shot Callie a slightly nervous glance in the mirror. "Um, are you having fun?"

Callie wondered if her feelings about George were more transparent than she'd hoped. Had even a casual acquaintance like Lorraine noticed how miserable she was? "Of course," she said cautiously. "Don't I look like I'm having fun?"

"Sorry." Lorraine smiled weakly. "Um, look Callie. I know we're not that close or anything. But I feel like I should say something, especially if you don't even know . . ." Her voice trailed off.

Callie turned to gaze at her, mystified. "What is it?" she demanded.

Lorraine lowered her brush and looked at Callie directly. "It's none of my business." She cleared her throat. "But I think you should know that a lot of people are talking about your family tonight. And most of what they're saying isn't very nice."

"What?" Callie swallowed hard, recalling all the curious glances aimed at her, the whispers and stares. "What are they saying?"

Lorraine shrugged, looking uncomfortable. "Stuff about Scott, mostly. About how it wasn't even his idea to get Fenton Hall invited to homecoming, but now he's taking all the credit for it. And, um, about how he was drinking at that party last weekend. And, well, I think I heard someone talking about your parents, too."

Callie gasped, wondering if her brother had any inkling about any of this. "What are they saying about my parents?"

"I don't really know." Lorraine seemed more uncomfortable than ever. As she spoke, she kept shooting little glances at the door. "Listen, I'd better get back to my date before he thinks I fell in." She smiled apologetically at Callie. "Anyway, I just thought you should know."

"I appreciate it," Callie said, not bothering to try to stop Lorraine as she scurried out of the bathroom.

She turned to face the mirror again, but this time she hardly saw her own reflection. Why did this sort of thing have to happen to her family so often? It seemed that there were far too many people out there who couldn't wait to chew over some juicy tidbit about the Foresters, whether or not it had any basis in truth. But why now? Why tonight?

Obviously, this must have something to do with the election, Callie told herself. *But who . . . ?*

Suddenly she gasped. She had begun her thought by considering Valerie Watkins and the other candidates running against Scott, but none of them seemed capable of a low trick like spreading rumors about their opposition. Then it occurred to her that there was another person with an ax to grind—a person who, according to all reports, was more than nasty enough to—

"Well, well," Veronica diAngelo commented, pushing open the bathroom door and strolling inside. "Look who's here. The great politician's sister." Her voice was dripping with sarcasm as she gazed at Callie through narrowed eyes.

Callie gritted her teeth. The last thing she felt like doing was confronting Veronica about this, at least before she spoke to Scott. *He mentioned that she was annoyed he wasn't taking her to this dance,* she thought. *I suppose I should have guessed that was the understatement of the year.*

"Hi, Veronica," she said as mildly as she could. "If you'll excuse me, I was just leaving."

"Whatever." Veronica stepped aside to let her pass, but she didn't take her eyes off Callie's face. "By the way, if you talk to your brother anytime soon, you might mention to him that the science club is always looking for new members. Because I suspect he may be looking around for a new extra-curricular activity sometime around, oh, say, Tuesday."

Callie didn't bother to answer. She hurried past Veronica, her heart pounding. She had to find Scott and let him know what was happening right away. Maybe he could still talk to Veronica, appease her somehow before this went any further.

"There you are, Callie," George said, eagerly stepping forward as she emerged from the bathroom. "I was hoping you'd come out before this song ended. It's one of my—"

"Sorry, George," Callie interrupted. She had almost forgotten about him, and at the moment she didn't have the patience to coddle him very much. "I've got to find Scott right away. I'll explain later, okay?"

She brushed past him and headed for the crowded dance floor, doing her best to ignore the hurt expression on his face.

Meanwhile, Carole was leaning against the rough wooden side wall of Samson's stall. She had been with the big black horse since leaving Lisa in the tack room a short while earlier, and as usual, just being in his presence made her feel a little calmer about things.

But that still didn't mean she knew what to do about her problem. "This is so hard," she said, speaking more to herself than to the horse. Samson's usual high energy had been lowered by their earlier workout, and he was standing quietly, chewing on a mouthful of hay while she watched him. "I really don't think I can decide this. It's too hard."

The horse clearly didn't have any answers for her, and Carole fell silent again, simply letting herself get caught up in watching him. It seemed so natural to stand there and look at the big black gelding, be with him, plan their next ride together. It felt natural and right and completely fulfilling. He was everything a horse could be and then some. In just two weeks she would ride him in the Colesford Horse Show, and after that, who knew what challenges waited on the horizon? The future seemed limitless with a horse so talented.

But it wasn't only Samson's show potential that thrilled her. It was Samson himself. She had been crazy about him since the moment he was born, and the better she got to know his courageous, willing spirit, the more she loved him. It was inconceivable that her future wouldn't involve him.

But it was equally inconceivable that it wouldn't contain Starlight. "I've got to go, fella," Carole whispered, stepping forward to give Samson a pat. "I'll see you later, okay?" He lifted his head from his hayrack and turned to blink at her. She smiled at the curious, sleepy expression on his face. Then, after giving him a few more pats, she let herself out into the stable aisle.

139

Starlight was sleeping when she reached his stall. "Hey, boy," she called softly from the aisle, not wanting to startle him.

He snorted and awakened instantly, moving forward to greet her as eagerly as always. She smiled as he shoved his big head over the half door and nuzzled at her shirt, obviously looking for treats.

"Sorry, boy," she said, rubbing his face and then pushing it back gently as she let herself into the stall. "No apples today." Once inside, she slipped her arms around his neck for a quick hug. "Maybe next time, okay?"

Pulling back, Carole ran her hand down the length of her horse's sleek, muscular back. His mahogany coat glowed with good health, and his glossy black mane lay smoothly along his slightly arched neck. Moving around to his front, she scratched him in his favorite places, taking in the familiar off-kilter shape of the white star splashed on his forehead and his bright, inquisitive, friendly eyes.

"You're such a good guy," Carole told Starlight softly, brushing a piece of straw out of his forelock. "You're such a big old good-hearted guy."

I remember the first day I saw him, she thought, smiling slightly at the memory. *I scratched him on the face to reassure him, and he nuzzled my neck.*

Starlight butted her shoulder with his nose, as if remembering that day along with her, and she automatically reached up to scratch him again in his fa-

140

vorite spot. He sighed with pleasure and let his eyelids droop, drooling slightly on her arm.

Carole bit her lip. Now that she had started this trip down memory lane, more special moments flooded into her mind. She thought about the way Judy Barker had tricked her into riding the gelding across the fields from his old stable to Pine Hollow, keeping the wonderful secret that Carole's father had already bought the horse for her as a Christmas gift. When Carole had found out the truth, she had been so overwhelmed that she'd hardly been able to believe it at first. She had wanted a horse of her very own for so long, and knowing that her dream had finally come true—and in such a wonderful way— had been one of the best moments of her life.

Tonight, being with her horse felt as comfortable as always. But was he still helping her grow as a rider, still changing her life? Or was there something missing now, something she had rediscovered with Samson?

I can't imagine my life without Starlight, she thought, stroking her horse's smooth cheek with her fingertips. *But it's not right to keep him around just because I can't bear to let go and move on.*

"You deserve a rider who's going to put you first," she murmured. She moved to stand directly in front of the horse, grabbed his big face in both hands, and looked at him steadily. "You're no second banana."

Starlight pricked his ears toward her curiously and snorted. Carole drank in the sight of him, memorizing every curve and angle of his head for the millionth time.

A moment later she felt something drip onto her arm, and she realized that tears were running down her cheeks. That was when she knew she'd made her decision.

TEN

"Ugh," Callie said, wrinkling her nose with distaste as she yanked something unidentifiable out of the drain of the kitchen sink. "It's times like this that I really wish Dad was still a lowly state legislator. It seems like we didn't have to do nearly as many disgusting chores back then."

Scott glanced up from scrubbing the stove top and chuckled. "I know what you mean," he said. "He's so hyped on the idea of us being a 'normal' family that it's practically abnormal. I'd hate to think what he'd want us to do if he ever decided to run for president."

Callie rolled her eyes. "It's hard to believe you can still laugh after what happened last night at the dance." She'd been feeling a bit grumpy all morning, and she suspected that her bad mood had sprung mostly from her own guilt about the way she had treated George the evening before. After her encounter with Veronica, Callie had managed to keep herself so busy dealing with Scott's problems that she hadn't spent any more time alone with George.

143

With Scott's help, she'd even been able to dodge the whole issue of a good-night kiss. Still, judging by the way George had stared longingly after her as Scott had bundled her into his car, Callie guessed that he probably hadn't gotten the hint. She had been expecting and dreading the almost inevitable call from him all morning.

"The dance," Scott said thoughtfully. "Yes, that was an interesting evening, I'll admit."

"Interesting?" Callie snorted. "Is that what you call it when one of your romantic rejects totally trashes your family to everyone she knows?"

Scott frowned slightly. "I must admit, I didn't think Veronica would react that way." He gave the stove another halfhearted swipe with his sponge. "I guess I underestimated how angry she would get."

"No kidding. Not to mention underestimating what she was capable of when she got that way."

"Right." Scott sighed and glanced at his sister again. "By the way, I really am sorry that you got caught up in this."

Slipping off her rubber gloves and reaching up to tighten her messy blond ponytail, Callie shrugged. "I know. Not your fault."

Still, she couldn't help wincing as she thought about some of the garbage Veronica had been spreading. While most of her rumors were focused on Scott, a few targeted the rest of the Forester family—innuendos about Mr. and Mrs. Forester's marriage, gossip about Callie's love life back in her old hometown, even a totally outrageous lie about both Forester kids being recovering drug addicts.

"I'm sure most of the kids at school are smart enough to ignore the stuff Veronica's saying," Scott said, his forehead creasing slightly with worry. "But still, I wish—"

He cut himself off as Mrs. Forester poked her head into the kitchen. "How's it going in here, you two?" she asked. "I want to get started on lunch soon."

Callie picked up her rubber gloves and tossed them into the bucket on the floor nearby. "We're finished, Mom."

"And starved," Scott added, dropping his sponge into the bucket and picking it up. "Lunch sounds great."

Mrs. Forester glanced around the clean kitchen, a pleased smile on her youthful, delicate-featured face. "Nice job, kids. Why don't you go set the table in the dining room? I'll have something ready in a jiff."

As her mother started rummaging around in the refrigerator, Callie collected her crutches from where she'd leaned them against the counter and swung out of the kitchen. Scott followed her toward the dining room just across the hall.

As she dug into the sideboard for utensils, Callie glanced toward her brother. "So what are you going to do about her?"

"Who, Mom? Let her make lunch, of course," Scott joked.

Callie rolled her eyes. "Very funny. I'm talking about Veronica, you nitwit."

"What can I do?" Scott shrugged helplessly. "I'm going to wait it out and hope Tuesday's election shows her that people aren't paying attention to her lies."

Callie didn't think that was a very satisfactory solution. But she had to admit that she didn't have a better one.

When Callie and Scott returned to the kitchen a few minutes later, they found a platter of sandwich fixings laid out. Their mother was busy making a pitcher of lemonade while their father rooted around in the refrigerator.

"What are you looking for, Dad?" Scott asked.

Congressman Forester looked up. "The spicy mustard."

Mrs. Forester bustled over and leaned into the refrigerator, coming up with a small brown jar. "Here it is."

"Ah!" Congressman Forester took the jar and planted a kiss on his wife's cheek. "You're a lifesaver, honey."

At that moment the doorbell rang faintly at the front of the house. "Who could that be?" Mrs. Forester wondered, glancing at her watch and then at her husband. "Are you expecting anyone?"

"No." Congressman Forester set the mustard on the table and headed for the hall. "I'll see who it is."

Scott picked up the lunch platter and carried it

toward the dining room while Mrs. Forester came over to Callie and pushed a strand of hair out of her face. "How's your leg feeling, sweetheart?" she asked gently. "All that dancing last night didn't tire you out too much, did it?

Callie shrugged. "It's okay." She appreciated her mother's concern, though sometimes it irritated her a little. After all, she had been an athlete before her accident—an endurance rider, accustomed to long, strenuous, difficult competitions requiring all kinds of strength and stamina. Maybe she was out of training for the moment, but that didn't mean she was some kind of fragile flower who might collapse after a night of dancing. "No problem."

"Good." Mrs. Forester tucked another strand of her daughter's hair behind her ear.

Feeling a little self-conscious, Callie tugged at her ponytail again. She suddenly realized that she probably looked a mess, especially standing beside her mother, who looked cool and perfect as always.

"Callie," Congressman Forester called from the front hall. "You have a guest."

"Really?" Callie exchanged a surprised glance with Scott, who had just returned from the dining room. She couldn't imagine who would be stopping by to see her at lunchtime on a Sunday. "Who is it?"

She found out as her father entered the kitchen. George Wheeler was right behind him. Holding back a gasp of dismay, Callie forced herself to smile at George even as her head swam with shock.

"Um, hi," she greeted him.

George had a bright smile on his flushed, moon-shaped face. If he noticed her messy hair or the stained old sweats she was wearing, his expression certainly didn't show it.

"Hi, Callie," he said eagerly. "I was just in the neighborhood, so I thought I'd stop by and tell you in person what a fun time I had last night at the dance."

Callie shot a glance at her brother, who looked just as startled as she was to see George in their house. "Um, thanks, George," she said uncertainly. "I had fun, too."

She couldn't believe that George was there. What in the world was he thinking? Even if he'd had no clue about her feelings the evening before, it had been only their first date—hardly the time for him to start dropping by unannounced.

If her parents thought there was anything odd about the visit, they weren't letting on. "George, we were just about to sit down for lunch," Mrs. Forester said. "Won't you join us? It's nothing fancy—just sandwiches—but there's plenty."

Callie gulped, wishing that her parents' knee-jerk hospitality could have faltered just this once. All she wanted was to get George out of her house as quickly as possible. What was she going to say to him during an entire meal, especially with her parents listening to every word?

"Thank you," George said eagerly, glancing at Callie. "Are you sure it's no trouble?"

"No trouble at all. Callie's friends are always welcome." Congressman Forester gestured toward the dining room. "Come on, why don't we get started? I'm famished."

Moments later an extra place had been set for George, and all five of them were seated around the big oak dining table. Callie felt as though she were moving through some sort of bad dream.

"So, George," Congressman Forester said politely. "I understand you're a Pine Hollow regular, too."

Mrs. Forester smiled. "Oh, yes, George. Callie is forever telling us what a wonderful rider you are."

Callie gripped the butter knife tightly in her fist. She could feel her facing blushing a deep crimson. She couldn't believe her mother had just said that—it made it sound as though Callie spent all her time gushing about George! If anything, she might have mentioned once or twice that George had been chosen to represent Pine Hollow at the Colesford Horse Show. That was the extent of it.

"Really?" George looked embarrassed but happy. "Well, she may be exaggerating just a little about that. But I do love to ride."

"Have you been riding at Pine Hollow long, George?" Congressman Forester asked, reaching for the mustard.

George accepted the lemonade pitcher Scott was passing to him. "Ever since my mother and I moved to Willow Creek a little over a year ago," he said. "But I've been riding since I was in third grade. I really love it."

Mrs. Forester turned to smile at her daughter. "Callie feels just the same way," she said. "Especially endurance riding, of course—that's her specialty, as I'm sure you know, George. But as long as there's a horse involved, she's happy. Isn't that right, Callie?"

"Uh, sure," Callie said, feeling annoyed—at George for coming to her house, at her parents for inviting him in and making him feel at home, and most of all at herself for not setting George straight the night before as she should have done.

Scott shot her a sympathetic glance and cleared his throat. "So, Dad," he said, "did you finish that speech you were writing last night?"

Callie breathed a sigh of relief as the topic shifted away from her and George. Still, she couldn't relax entirely. She knew she was going to have to figure out what to do about the George situation, and fast. For the time being, though, all she could do was concentrate on her food and do her best to ignore the fact that George was spending most of his time gazing at her with that goofy smile on his face.

This is a nightmare, she told herself, thinking back wistfully to her quiet, peaceful morning of chores. *I'd rather have to clean out every disgusting drain in the house than sit here and deal with this.*

———

"Get away!" Stevie said in annoyance, shoving Bear toward the powder room door. "It's bad enough that I have to clean out every disgusting drain in the house without you sticking your big nose in here trying to help me."

Giving her a slightly wounded look, Bear turned and padded out of the tiny room beneath the stairs. Lowering himself to the hall floor with a sigh, he rested his face on his front paws and stared at Stevie mournfully.

Stevie ignored the dog. She had been feeling increasingly fidgety and anxious as the morning wore on, and she continued to wonder what had happened at the previous night's big dance. *Would it be too much to ask for Scott to call and let me know how it went?* she wondered peevishly, grabbing the chopstick she was using to pry the drain loose. *Or was Veronica's revenge so horrible that he just up and moved to Timbuktu overnight?*

She sighed, feeling frustrated and wishing she could just pick up the phone and find out. But she knew better than to try it. Her parents had been fairly reasonable about allowing her and Alex to accept occasional calls even though they were grounded, but they had made it clear that there were to be no outgoing calls without their express permission. And since Alex had spent most of the morning whining about wanting to call Lisa, and their parents had repeatedly refused the request, looking more annoyed each time, Stevie was pretty sure that it would be hopeless for her even to ask.

Fortunately, she had an alternate plan in mind. When the phone still hadn't rung by the time she poured the last drop of bleach down the powder room drain, she washed her hands and headed outside to find her parents.

Mr. Lake was nowhere to be seen, but Stevie soon located her mother in the backyard, planting bulbs in a flower bed near the swimming pool. "All drains clear and ready for action, ma'am," Stevie announced sharply, snapping into the crisp salute Carole's father, a retired Marine Corps colonel, had taught her years earlier. "Request permission to report to Pine Hollow."

Mrs. Lake glanced up and brushed a strand of blond hair off her forehead. "Very amusing, Stevie," she said, not looking particularly amused. "I know you think your father and I are running you ragged with these chores, but remember, it's only—"

"I know, I know," Stevie interrupted. "I'm sorry. I was just kidding around, really." She smiled appeasingly at her mother. "So, can I go to Pine Hollow and practice for a while?"

"I suppose so." Mrs. Lake glanced at her watch. "But make sure you're back here by two. Your father wants you and Alex to help him winterize the pool this afternoon."

"Okay." Stevie shrugged. Getting the pool ready for winter would actually have to rank as one of the pleasanter tasks her parents had found for her and Alex in the past week. "No problem. Thanks, Mom."

She hurried off before her mother could change her mind and decide she wanted her to paint the house or rotate the tires on her car before she left. Breaking into a jog as she hit the driveway, Stevie started on the familiar path to the stable, enjoying the feeling of relative freedom.

By the time she reached Pine Hollow less than ten minutes later, her mood had already improved. She was eager to get to work with Belle—after all, the horse show was now less than two weeks away, and she wanted to be ready—but first she had to get some answers about the dance.

She hurried into the stable building, glancing around for anyone who could tell her what she needed to know. But the place was relatively quiet for a weekend. Max was giving his five-year-old daughter, Maxi, a riding lesson in the schooling ring. Red was hosing down the entry hall. A pair of intermediate riders was just setting out on a trail ride. There was no sign of anyone who might have been at the homecoming dance. In fact, the only person Stevie saw who was anywhere near her age was Ben Marlow, who was cooling out a horse in the indoor ring, and she knew there was no chance he'd had a hot date to the big dance.

Stevie frowned, feeling disappointed. "Oh well," she muttered as she headed for the tack room.

Maybe someone would be around by the time she and Belle finished their practice session.

After grabbing her tack from its usual spot, Stevie walked back down the hall and across the entryway. Red had just finished his task, and he nodded at Stevie as he coiled his hose. Stevie waved back, but she didn't slow down. She had less than two hours before she had to be home, and she didn't want to waste a minute.

Entering the stable aisle, Stevie saw that it, too, was empty of other people. As she approached Belle's stall, she started to hear an odd sound among the familiar noises of the horses moving around in their stalls. For a moment she thought it must be Red's portable radio playing softly somewhere nearby. But as she took a step closer, she realized that it was the sound of muffled sobbing—and that it was coming from Starlight's stall.

Pausing just long enough to pat her mare on the nose, Stevie walked to Starlight's stall and peered inside. The bay gelding was standing in the middle of the stall with his gaze trained on Stevie. "Hello?" she said hesitantly. "Carole, are you in there?"

The noise stopped, and Stevie heard a gulp. "S-Stevie?" a weak voice said a few seconds later.

Leaning forward, Stevie looked directly down and saw her friend huddled against the back of the stall door. Carole's face was tilted upward, staring back at her through red-rimmed eyes. Her face was streaked with tears.

Stevie gasped. "What's the matter?"

Carole sniffled and wiped her cheek with the back of one hand. "Nothing." Her voice was almost inaudible.

Stevie wasn't about to take that as an answer. "Move over," she ordered. "I'm coming in." Without waiting for a response, she unlatched the stall door and stepped inside.

Carole was sitting up straighter, blinking rapidly and looking absolutely miserable. "I told you," she said. "I'm okay."

"Don't be ridiculous." Stevie patted Starlight quickly, then dropped to the floor of the stall beside Carole. "Now, come on. What's going on?"

Carole rubbed her nose, her dark eyes looking sad and frightened at the same time. "I don't want to talk about it."

Now Stevie knew this had to be serious. "Come on," she said. "Maybe I can help."

Carole shook her head and her eyes filled with tears. "It's not that kind of problem," she whispered.

"Carole." Stevie scooted closer and grabbed her friend's hands in her own. "Please. Whatever's wrong, you'll feel better if you talk about it. Here I am. So talk."

Carole swallowed hard. Then she glanced up at the bay horse standing quietly in the stall a few feet away. "It's about Starlight," she said in a tiny, strangled voice. "I—I decided I have to sell him."

Stevie gasped, and her head swam crazily.

"What?" she asked, suddenly wondering if she was in the middle of some kind of dream. She pulled one hand away from Carole's just long enough to give herself a hard pinch on the leg. No such luck—this was real life, all right. "What do you mean?" she asked, rubbing her leg and telling herself she must have misheard. "You mean you don't want him anymore?"

"It's not that." Carole hesitated, glancing at the horse once again.

"Is this some kind of money issue?" Stevie asked. She knew as well as anyone that owning a horse was an expensive proposition. She'd been under the impression that Colonel Hanson had been doing quite well financially since retiring from the military, but maybe she was wrong. "I mean, if you're having trouble making ends meet, I'm sure we could figure out a way to—"

Carole shook her head. "It's not about money," she broke in, pulling her hands away from Stevie and rubbing her eyes. "It's got nothing to do with that."

"What, then?"

"Well, do you remember that joke you made the other day? You know, about how I should get rid of Starlight and ask Dad to buy Samson for me instead?"

Stevie had no idea what she was talking about. "Did I say that?" she said blankly. "I don't remember. But anyway, I'm sure if I did I didn't really mean it."

156

"I know." Carole blinked and sniffled again. But her voice was stronger now. "Still, it started me thinking. And then I started talking to Ben, and then to Lisa . . . Well, anyway, I realized I've been spending most of my time with Samson, even when I don't have to. Time that I used to spend with Starlight. Don't you see?"

Stevie wasn't sure she did. She was shocked to the core to hear Carole talking like this. She and Starlight were a pair—a perfect match. "But—"

"It's not like I *want* to give him up," Carole said. "But if I can't give him the attention he deserves anymore, isn't it the only choice?"

Stevie was finally starting to see what Carole was getting at, though she was still having a difficult time believing it. "So you're really going to do it?" she said. "Sell Starlight and buy Samson from Max?"

"I haven't gotten to that second part yet." Carole bit her lip and picked at the straw covering the stall floor, rolling a small piece between her fingers. "All I know is that Samson is the one I think about all the time these days. Starlight should have someone thinking about him that way, and if I'm not doing it, I need to find someone who will."

"Wow." Stevie was silent for a moment, struggling to fit this bombshell into her worldview somehow so that it made sense. Starlight had always belonged to Carole heart and soul—how could she care more for another horse, even a special one like Samson, than she did about her own? Stevie didn't know, but she could tell by the haggard look in Carole's eyes that there could be no mistake. "This is huge."

"I know. But don't tell anyone else, okay, please?" Carole begged. A tear trickled out of the corner of her eye and traced its way slowly down her cheek. "I can't bear to have anyone else know about this yet, not even Dad or Max."

"You haven't told anyone?"

Carole shrugged. "Well, Lisa knows I've been thinking about this. And I'm pretty sure Ben has guessed what I decided, but you know how he is. He isn't prying."

Stevie nodded. "You know you can trust me," she said. "I won't breathe a word."

"Thanks." Carole smiled weakly as a few more tears squeezed out. "You were right. I do feel a little better now that I've talked about it."

"You don't look much better," Stevie said bluntly. She moved a little closer, until she could reach over and give Carole a hug. "Isn't there anything else I can do to help?"

Carole clung to her for a moment before letting go. "Just one thing," she said, her voice breaking as Starlight wandered over and snuffled at her hair with his nose. "You can help me find a buyer for him."

Stevie glanced up at the horse, feeling her own eyes well up. "Of course," she said, blinking back the tears along with her own reluctance to do what Carole was asking. This wasn't the time to start blubbering—she needed to be strong for Carole's sake. No matter how much she hated the idea of the lively bay gelding possibly leaving Pine Hollow, she had to stand by her friend's painful decision. "I'll do whatever I can."

"Thanks."

As the two friends sat silently for a moment, watching Starlight move around in his stall, Stevie found herself wondering why she hadn't had the slightest inkling that this was coming. *Am I getting out of touch with my friends?* she wondered, feeling a twinge of guilt. *I have been awfully busy lately with everything that's been going on—the horse show, the election—and getting myself grounded hasn't helped.*

"Listen, Carole," she said, not certain how to express what she was thinking. "I'm really sorry I didn't realize you were thinking about this. I mean, I wish I'd been paying closer attention, you know, so maybe I could have helped sooner."

Carole was already shaking her head. "Don't worry," she assured her. "You're not the only one this took by surprise. I had no clue it was coming myself until, well, yesterday, I guess."

"Oh." That only made Stevie feel a tiny bit better. She still couldn't quite believe that this wasn't all some kind of weird nightmare. But this time, she didn't need to pinch herself. The pain in her heart as she looked at Starlight was real enough to convince her.

ELEVEN

Stevie was still thinking about Carole's announcement when she walked across her driveway at exactly three minutes before two. Her talk with Carole had meant she'd only had time for a short session with Belle, but it was just as well. After their little talk, Stevie had been too distracted to accomplish much that day anyway.

I can't believe she's serious about this, Stevie thought as she headed for the front door. *I still don't really understand how it happened, especially right under my nose like that. It came totally out of the blue.*

But when she thought back over the past couple of months, Stevie realized that that wasn't really true. There had been occasional moments, ever since Samson's arrival at Pine Hollow, when Stevie had noticed that Carole was spending an awful lot of time with the big black horse. But it hadn't happened often enough for her to start to wonder about it consciously, let alone put two and two together and figure out what was happening. Or maybe she just hadn't been paying enough attention because of

160

all the other things that had been going on at the same time—the start of school, all the problems that Phil's best friend, A.J., had been going through, the news about the horse show, the election campaign, Lisa's fight with Alex and everything else that had happened at the party. It had really been a busy autumn, and it wasn't over yet.

Still, Stevie planned to do whatever she could to help Carole through this difficult time. If that meant helping her locate a new owner for Starlight, well, she would just have to find the best darn owner in the entire world—aside from Carole herself, of course. During the walk home, Stevie had already come up with a short list of possibilities, including a friend of her older brother's, an acquaintance or two from Fenton Hall, and a summer intern from her mother's law firm. She didn't know if any of them would pan out, but she planned to talk to each of them as soon as possible, along with anyone else she could think of. If Carole had her mind made up, there was no sense dragging things out any longer than necessary. That would only make things harder for all of them.

As she passed the garage, Stevie saw that her mother's green hatchback was missing from its usual spot. She also spotted Alex in the side yard raking leaves.

"Hi," Stevie called, hurrying toward him. "Where did Mom go?"

Alex stopped what he was doing and leaned on his

rake. "She and Dad went to the grocery store," he said. "They just left with Michael a few minutes ago."

"Oh, well," Stevie commented. "I'm sure they left us a couple of chores to do so we wouldn't be bored, right?"

"Bingo." Alex grinned and started raking again.

Stevie headed for the door. When she pushed it open, she heard the phone ringing from inside. With a gasp, she realized that she'd never gotten any answers about the dance—in fact, in all her agitation over Carole's big decision, she'd forgotten all about it. But now her curiosity bubbled up again. Maybe Scott was finally calling to let her know what had happened.

She raced around the corner into the living room and lunged for the phone on the end table by the sofa. "Hello?" she blurted out.

"Stevie? Is that you?" Phil's voice queried from the other end of the line.

Stevie went limp, flopping onto the sofa. "Yeah, it's me," she said. "What's up?"

"Not much. What have you been up to today?"

Stevie shrugged off her jacket and tossed it over the arm of a nearby wing chair, suddenly remembering their rather testy conversation the day before. She guessed that Phil was calling to touch base, make sure there were no hard feelings. "I just got home from Pine Hollow," she said, wishing she could tell him about Carole's news. But she had promised to keep quiet until Carole was ready to let people know, and she intended to keep that promise. "Otherwise, more of the same—work, work, work."

"You won't get in trouble for talking to me now, will you?" Phil sounded worried.

"Nope. Mom and Dad are out," Stevie replied, propping her feet up on the coffee table. "So have you talked to anyone who went to the Willow Creek dance last night?"

"No," Phil replied. "Why? Did something exciting happen?"

"I wish I knew." Stevie frowned. "I'm sure Veronica must have at least tried to get back at Scott for dumping her. But nobody has bothered to call and tell me what she did." She sneaked a glance at her watch, wondering if she should risk trying to call Scott despite her parents' ban. She wished she'd thought to ask Alex whether they'd just gone to pick up a couple of things or if they'd had a long list. That would give her a better idea of how much time she had before their return.

"Maybe that means nothing happened," Phil suggested.

Stevie snorted. "Fat chance," she said. "This is Veronica we're talking about, remember? And she pretty much came right out and threatened to sabotage the election the other day. I heard it myself."

"Whatever." Phil didn't sound very interested. "So anyway, how was Belle today? Are you guys going to be ready for the big show?"

"Sure," Stevie said dismissively, her mind still focused on Scott and Veronica. "I wonder if she actually would have the gall to pay people to vote her way?"

"You mean Belle?" Phil asked lightly. "I really don't think she wants a blue ribbon that badly."

Stevie rolled her eyes. "Very funny," she said. "Quit kidding around, okay? This is serious. If Veronica pulls something big enough, it could cost Scott the whole election."

"What a tragedy," Phil said dryly. "Excuse me while I get a tissue."

Stevie frowned. "You could at least pretend to be supportive here, you know," she snapped. "This is important to me."

"I can tell," Phil shot back. "It's taking up enough of your time."

"What do you mean by that?"

"Nothing." Phil sounded wounded. "It just kind of seems like this stupid election is all you ever talk about these days."

Stevie blinked in disbelief. "What?"

"You heard me. You might as well just start going out with Scott Forester. He sees a whole lot more of you than I do, that's for sure."

She couldn't believe that Phil was acting like such a jerk all of a sudden. Didn't he realize how much she had going on in her life these days? "You've got to be kidding!" she exclaimed. "In case it's slipped your mind, I'm grounded, remember? But in spite of

164

that, I'm trying my best to do a good job running this campaign. *And* deal with Veronica. *And* prepare for a major horse show. *And* help my friends with their problems. Not to mention keeping up with my schoolwork so my parents don't ground me all over again when they see my next report card." She paused just long enough to take a deep breath. "So *pardon me* if I'm not rushing over to hold your hand every day and your male ego's feeling insecure about it."

"Fine," Phil said coldly. "Whatever. My sister needs to use the phone." With a click, the connection cut off and the dial tone buzzed in Stevie's ear.

She lowered the receiver and stared at it in shock, as if it were a butterfly that had suddenly transformed into a poisonous spider. She could hardly believe that Phil had actually hung up on her. Her first instinct was to call him right back, but she hesitated.

"Why should I?" she muttered. "He's the one who's being immature here."

She couldn't believe he'd actually made that snide comment about Scott. Since when was he the kind of boyfriend who turned into a jealous, raving lunatic whenever she passed another guy on the street? They had always trusted each other. Why had he decided to stop now?

It was too strange—she had to call him back and find out what had gotten into him. She had her hand on the receiver, ready to pick it up and dial, when it rang shrilly. She jumped and yanked her hand back, startled. Then, realizing it was probably Phil calling back to apologize for hanging up on her, she answered quickly. "Hello?"

"Stevie? Hey, how's it going? It's Scott."

"Oh. Hi," Stevie replied, doing her best to sound normal. "It's about time you called. I've been dying of curiosity—what happened with Veronica last night?"

"Plenty," Scott said ruefully. "I think we need to do some strategizing to get ready for school tomorrow. Do you have time to talk now?"

"Absolutely." Pushing her conversation with Phil out of her mind, Stevie focused her attention on Scott. "Now tell me what happened."

Carole had meant it when she'd told Stevie she felt better after talking about her decision. In the hours since their conversation, she had mostly been able to keep her emotions under control. But she still got a knot in her stomach every time she looked at Starlight or thought about what she'd decided to do. She had longed him for half an hour in a secluded schooling ring behind the stable building, not trusting herself to ride him or work him in public. After untacking him and giving him a quick grooming, she had left him in his stall and done her best to distract herself from her grief by taking care of other chores.

She was almost relieved when Max tracked her

down as she was leading Prancer in from the paddock and asked her to help Ben and him do the weekly task that he called hall monitoring. Normally sweeping cobwebs out of the rafters and raking down the stable aisles were among Carole's least favorite chores, but today the idea of throwing herself into mindless physical labor was a welcome relief.

"Lead the way," she told Max. "I'll show those spiders who's boss."

Max looked a bit surprised at her enthusiasm, but he nodded. "Ben's getting the tools," he said. "We'll start in the indoor ring. Once Prancer's settled in, come meet us there."

Carole did as he said, returning Prancer to her stall and checking her water bucket before hurrying to meet the others. It was still early enough that many of the horses were outside, either grazing in the pastures and paddocks or on the trail with weekend riders. It was the perfect time to clean up and get things nice and neat for the coming week.

Max was already raking the floor of the large indoor ring, concentrating on the track around the perimeter, which had been worn into a shallow rut by dozens of hooves over the past seven days. Ben had filled a bucket with water and was rinsing a manure stain off the wall near the ring's double doors. Carole grabbed the broom leaning nearby and smiled at him tentatively.

"Hi," she said. She and Ben hadn't spoken much since their conversation on Friday evening, and after everything that had come of that last talk, she felt a little shy with him. "Looks like you're taking a real working holiday today."

"Looks like," Ben replied mildly, not looking up from his task. Sunday was technically Ben's day off, but more often than not he stopped by the stable to do a few chores anyway. Carole had never found that particularly strange—rarely a day went by when she didn't spend at least an hour or two at Pine Hollow, whether she really needed to be there or not. But once she'd found out where he lived, Carole had been even less surprised that Ben preferred the stable to his home. She couldn't imagine spending any more time than she had to in that drab, dingy, depressing little shack that he shared with his grandfather.

Carole moved away and brushed at a dusty cobweb dangling from the edge of the wooden door. The ceiling of the indoor ring was too high to reach, so she concentrated on the doorway and walls, banishing every cobweb she could find.

By the time she'd finished, the others had completed their jobs as well. "Come on," Max said. "Time to move on."

Carole and Ben picked up their cleaning supplies and followed without a word. Soon they were repeating their tasks in the entryway, and then in one arm of the U-shaped stable aisle.

Throwing herself into her work had made Carole feel a little better at first. But when she was once again in sight of Starlight's stall, her stomach started to tie itself in knots and her eyes started to burn with unshed tears. She carefully kept her gaze trained on the rafters and her broom, not looking in the direction of the stall in question. But as the three of them worked their way closer and closer, it got harder to keep from peeking. Soon they were only six doors down from Starlight's stall, then five, then four . . .

"Carole," Max said suddenly, breaking into her concentration. Glancing at him, she saw that he had half a dozen water buckets dangling from his hands, and several more sat at his feet. He had been removing them from the stalls as they went along. "Can you give me a hand here? I want to get these outside before someone comes along and trips over them. We can rinse them out later."

Carole bit her lip and glanced at the doorway at the far end of the aisle. "Um, okay," she agreed reluctantly, leaning over to pick up the rest of the buckets.

I can do this, she told herself sternly. *I can walk past his stall without freaking out and letting Max know something's going on. I know I can.*

Max started down the aisle, and she followed with her eyes focused carefully on his back. But she'd hardly taken half a dozen steps toward the door when she heard an all-too-familiar snort from just ahead. Her eyes danced toward the sound, and the sight that greeted them was so familiar, so sweet and touching, that tears sprang to her eyes once again.

Starlight had heard them coming and was standing at the front of his stall with his long neck stretched over the half door. His eyes were bright, his ears were pricked forward alertly, and his head was tilted just slightly to one side. It was a mischievous, welcoming look.

Carole stopped short, unable to take another step, and simply stared at her horse while simultaneous waves of love and anguish washed over her, nearly bowling her over. One of the buckets dropped from her hand and clattered against the floor.

Max turned at the noise. "Carole?" he said when he saw her standing there staring at her horse. "What are you doing?"

Carole couldn't answer. She wanted to—she knew she had to say something soon or Max would figure out that something was going on. But her mouth wouldn't work, and she couldn't tear her eyes away from the bay horse just a few yards away. What was more, hot tears were seriously threatening to spill over. If she so much as blinked, she knew there was no way she would be able to stop their flow.

"Carole?" Max said more loudly, taking a step toward her. "Are you all right? You look kind of—"

At that moment there was a shout from farther back down the aisle. "Uh-oh!" Ben exclaimed.

Carole finally worked up the strength to tear her gaze away from Starlight, and she and Max both turned to look. Ben was standing where they'd left him, but somehow he'd managed to kick over his cleaning bucket, sending dirty water spilling across the aisle, splattering on the walls, and seeping into a couple of nearby stalls.

"Oh, man," Max muttered, dropping the buckets he was holding and hurrying toward Ben.

"Sorry," Ben called, smiling sheepishly at Max. "Don't know what got into me. Just lost track of my feet."

Carole goggled at Ben, so surprised that she forgot her own problems for a second. It wasn't like Ben to be so clumsy. It wasn't like him at all.

Suddenly she realized what had happened. Ben had done it on purpose. He had caused a commotion intentionally to distract Max, because he'd seen how upset Carole was and guessed that she didn't want to tell Max why. Her theory was confirmed a moment later when Max leaned over to retrieve the tipped cleaning bucket and Ben shot her a look of concern over his shoulder.

I can't believe it, Carole thought. *He did it for me. He made himself look like a total idiot to help me out.*

She felt surprised and confused and grateful all at once. Ben was really coming through for her these days, being a true friend. After what had happened between them at the party the previous weekend, she had doubted their friendship would ever get back on track. In fact, she hadn't been sure she would ever be able to look him in the face again. But now that the chips were down, she was learning that Ben just might be someone she could count on after all.

Still, she didn't have much energy to think about that at the moment. She had to pull herself together before Max remembered her weird behavior and asked her about it again. She cleared her throat, keeping her eyes averted from Starlight, who was still curiously watching all the action in the aisle. "I'll take care of these," she called to the others, gathering up as many of the buckets as she could carry. "Be right back."

Without waiting for their reply, she made her escape, hurrying down the aisle and out the back door into the cool November afternoon. Dropping the buckets by the outdoor spigot, she pressed the heels of her palms against her eyes, taking several deep breaths.

When she felt a little more in control of her own emotions, she allowed herself to think about what had just happened. *That was a close call,* she told herself. *If I want to keep this secret for more than two seconds, I'm going to have to handle things a lot better than I just did.*

She knew she was also going to have to thank Ben for coming to her rescue. She vowed to do so as soon as she could.

TWELVE

The next morning Lisa took a different route than she usually did, turning left on Magnolia Street instead of driving straight along Old Town Road to the high school. As she waited for the light to change at the intersection of Magnolia and Broad streets, the closest thing Willow Creek had to a main drag, she glanced at the seat beside her. A long white envelope lay there, a stamp perfectly aligned in the upper right-hand corner.

Lisa smiled and turned her attention back to the road. She had decided to take this roundabout route because she wanted to stop by the post office and mail the envelope, which contained her acceptance of NVU's offer for her to join the next year's freshman class. It was all filled out and signed. All she had to do was mail it to make it official.

I can't wait to see the look on Alex's face when I tell him about this, she thought happily, pressing down gently on the gas pedal as the station wagon in front of her crept slowly across the intersection. *He's going to be almost as excited about it as I am.*

She had already decided to wait to share the news until she could do so in person. That might not be anytime soon, unfortunately, since he was grounded. But she knew it would be worth the wait.

Once he finds out, there's no way he'll mind my spending a measly little week in California over Thanksgiving, she told herself.

Thinking about California reminded her of her most recent conversation with her father. He had called the evening before to say hi, and Lisa had caught a few hints that made her think he might be planning to tell her sooner than she'd thought that he was buying Prancer for her. She had expected him to wait with the news until graduation, but now she wasn't so sure. Why else would he mention three times in a twenty-minute conversation that there might be some surprises waiting for her in California? He'd pretended he was talking about the nice weather, or a new coat of paint on the porch, or how much Lily had grown. But Lisa knew her father well enough to realize that he was probably just too pleased about his special gift to keep it a secret much longer.

She hit her turn signal, preparing to pull into the drive-through lane of the post office. *Well, Dad may a have a big surprise for me,* she thought with a smile as she pulled up to the row of big blue mailboxes and rolled down her window, squinting in the bright morning sunlight bouncing off her car's side mirror. *But I've got one for him, too.* She was really looking forward to telling him that she'd settled on a college already. *Of course,* she added, her smile fading slightly, *at some point before that I'll have to find a time to tell Mom.*

Sliding her letter into the narrow, grimacing mouth of the mailbox, she prepared to drive on, thinking about her mother's behavior that weekend. Lisa had planned to tell Mrs. Atwood about her momentous decision as soon as she'd arrived home from Pine Hollow on Saturday night. But Rafe had still been there, and Lisa didn't want to share the news with him—especially since he was a student at NVU himself. When she'd remembered that, it had been the only dark spot on her positive feelings about her choice.

Of course, he'll probably flunk out by the time I get there next year, she comforted herself as she pulled out of the post office driveway and headed for school. *Especially if he keeps spending so much time with Mom when he should probably be studying.*

She wrinkled her nose as she remembered how, on Sunday, her mother had gone out with Rafe right after they'd both finished their shifts at the store. Mrs. Atwood had called at nine P.M. to tell Lisa that she and Rafe had decided to drive to Washington, D.C., for a romantic dinner, and they wouldn't be back until late. A whim, Mrs. Atwood had called it.

Mom never used to have whims before she hooked up with that greasy-haired underage dork, Lisa thought sourly. She shook her head, trying to banish her negative thoughts. This was supposed to be a happy day. Her future was rosy—she'd chosen a college, she was getting the horse of her dreams, and her boyfriend was going to be very happy very soon. What difference did it make, really, if her mother hadn't been around to hear about it exactly when Lisa had wanted her to be?

Anyway, it's not like I don't have plenty of time to break the news. Lisa's smile crept back, and she squeezed the steering wheel excitedly as she thought about all the people this decision would make happy. *And when I do tell her, she's going to be almost as excited as I am!*

Across town at Fenton Hall, Callie had hardly entered the school building when she saw George hurrying toward her with a big smile on his face.

"Callie!" he exclaimed breathlessly as he reached her side. "I was waiting for you. Can I carry your books?"

For a second Callie wondered if she'd heard him right. He could see perfectly well that her schoolbooks were in the backpack strapped onto her shoulders. That left both hands free to operate her crutches, and it was a system that worked very well. But he seemed to be stuck in some kind of cheesy 1950s time warp—didn't he know that girls these days were perfectly happy to carry their own books?

"Um, no thanks," Callie said through clenched teeth. "I've got it covered."

"Okay." George fell into step beside her as she continued toward her homeroom. "So listen, I wanted to say again how much fun I had at the dance, Callie."

Callie cringed. His voice was so loud that several other students in the hall turned to glance at them curiously. What had happened to the shy, soft-spoken George she'd gotten to know at Pine Hollow and in chemistry class? She didn't know, but this new, pushy George was really wearing on her nerves. The day before, she'd feared it was going to take a stick of dynamite to get him out of her house. He had stayed for more than two hours, chatting with her parents and insisting on helping Callie and Scott clean up after lunch. If the Foresters hadn't had to leave to visit an elderly great-aunt in a nearby nursing home, Callie wasn't sure George ever would have left.

"Thanks, George," Callie said as patiently as she could. She knew that this was partly her fault—she never should have let him go on thinking he had a chance with her after the dance, not even for a couple of days. Any other guy would have taken the hint after she'd dodged that kiss on Saturday night, not to mention slow-dancing with another guy during their date, but George just didn't seem to be catching on.

"So how was your trip to see your great-aunt yesterday afternoon?" George continued chattily. "Is

177

her cold any better? From what your mother said, it sounded like it was a bad one."

"Fine. She's fine." Callie forced herself to smile, ignoring still more curious glances as she looked around desperately for Scott. He had dropped her off at the front steps before going on to park the car. Maybe he would come in soon and rescue her from George.

Instead, Callie saw Stevie rushing toward her, her dark blond hair flying every which way and her cheeks pink. "Callie!" Stevie called breathlessly. "Wait up!"

Callie was happy to obey. She stopped short, half hoping that George wouldn't notice and would keep walking along, talking loudly to himself. But he stopped, too.

"Hi, Stevie," Callie said. "What's going on?"

Stevie skidded to a halt in front of her. "Bad stuff," she announced. "Where's Scott?"

"On his way," Callie reported. "Why? Did something else happen?" She already knew that Veronica's rumor mill had stayed busy over the weekend—Scott had received more than a dozen calls from friends reporting things they'd heard.

Stevie suddenly glanced at George, who was still standing beside Callie. "Listen, George," she said, "could you excuse us a minute? I need to talk to Callie."

"That's okay," George said eagerly. "If there's something going on, maybe I could help, or—"

"I don't think so." Stevie's voice was curt. "This is kind of private. Sorry." She didn't sound sorry at all. Turning her back on George, she jerked her head toward the girls' bathroom. "Come on."

Even George couldn't miss that kind of hint. He watched forlornly as Stevie dragged Callie toward the rest room. Callie felt a twinge of guilt, but it was more than overtaken by relief as she hurried after Stevie and away from George.

Stevie didn't pay any attention to George whatsoever as she raced toward the bathroom, pausing long enough to let Callie catch up on her crutches. Opening the girls' room door, she glanced inside, hoping it wouldn't be too crowded. Luckily, it was early enough that there were only a couple of people inside, washing their hands or checking their makeup in the mirror. Leading the way to a quiet spot around the corner beyond the row of stalls, Stevie turned to Callie.

"This is a disaster," she said. "Veronica is totally on a rampage."

Callie shrugged. "Tell me something I don't know. People were calling our house all weekend wanting to know stuff like if Scott had ever been to the Betty Ford Center and if it was true that my dad hired a hit man to kill off his opponent in his last election."

"But it's even worse than that," Stevie said urgently, tapping one foot impatiently on the tile floor. She had arrived at school early that morning, drag-

179

ging Alex away from his breakfast after only one bowl of cornflakes so that she would have extra time to gauge the voters' reactions to Veronica's gossip. It hadn't taken her long to discover that the situation was dire indeed. "Spreading rumors wasn't enough for her. Now she's actively campaigning for Valerie."

Callie raised her eyebrows. "Really? I didn't know they were friends."

"They're not. That's not the point. She doesn't care about Valerie winning—she just wants Scott to lose, and she knows Val's his only serious competition."

"I see." Callie shrugged. "So what are we supposed to do about it? Veronica can campaign for anyone she wants, and we can't stop her—free speech and all that, you know. Even if her motives are rotten."

Stevie didn't think Callie fully appreciated the gravity of the situation. Glancing at the row of sinks, she saw that the primpers had left and she and Callie were alone in the bathroom. "But she's not just campaigning," she protested. "She's spreading all kinds of lies and exaggerations, too, like telling anyone who'll listen that it was all *her* idea to combine our fall dance with Willow Creek's homecoming."

"Wasn't it?" Callie asked quietly.

Stevie frowned. "Maybe at first," she argued. "But Scott was the one who made it happen. Isn't that what politicians are supposed to do? Take action and make people's ideas become reality? Isn't that why we're calling Scott the action candidate?"

"Sure," Callie said reasonably. "Don't get me wrong, I'm not saying I agree with what Veronica's doing. I'm just trying to tell you that sometimes there's not much you can do about that sort of negative campaigning except try to rise above it."

"What?" Stevie didn't like the sound of that. It sounded too much like rolling over and letting Veronica get away with it, and that wasn't an idea she relished. Veronica got away with too much as it was—just because she was pretty and rich, she acted as if the world owed her whatever she wanted. "But she's making people think that Scott is just, like, her puppet or something. That he didn't have anything to do with making the dance happen. What if people actually believe that?"

"I doubt they will," Callie replied. "Dad ran into the same kind of thing in a few of his campaigns, and he won most of them anyway."

Stevie was about to respond, but at that moment the bathroom door swung open. Leaning forward to see who it was, Stevie saw Valerie Watkins enter with several friends. Valerie spotted Stevie and Callie right away.

"Hello," she greeted them politely, pushing her glasses farther up her nose. "Callie, I don't know what's going on, but I just want you to know that I don't have anything to do with all those rumors that are flying around."

Callie smiled back. "Thanks, Valerie, I—"

"Yeah, thanks," Stevie interrupted. "Now how about getting Veronica to back off, since she's doing this out of some kind of misguided effort to help you?"

Valerie looked at Stevie in surprise. "I don't know what you're talking about, Stevie, but I didn't ask Veronica to do anything."

Callie spoke up quickly. "Stevie and I know that, Valerie. It's just that we're both a little upset. It's not fun having people talk about you behind your back. Especially when it's all lies."

"I guess politics can get ugly even at the high-school level," Valerie replied. "I'm really sorry about what's going on, and sorry that you got caught up in it."

"Thanks again," Callie said. "Come on, Stevie, I'm going to be late for class if I don't get a move on."

Stevie looked like she wanted to say something more to Valerie, but instead she just nodded politely and followed Callie out the door. She and Callie could continue their conversation later, when they could get some privacy. In the meantime, she had to start thinking of some way to negate what Veronica was doing.

Stevie was so busy campaigning during first period that her Spanish teacher spoke sharply to her three times for talking during class. By the third time, Stevie wasn't even sure exactly what Señora Johnson was saying anymore—her long-winded rebuke went way beyond Stevie's knowledge of Spanish vocabulary. Still, she figured at that point that she'd better control herself before her teacher remembered the Spanish word for "detention."

As soon as Señora Johnson released the class at the end of the period, Stevie leaped out of her seat, quickly gathered her books and papers into a messy pile, and hurried out of the room. She had a few minutes before she had to report to her math classroom, and she planned to make the most of it.

"Hey, Betsy," she said, spotting Betsy Cavanaugh heading down the hall to her next class. Stevie grabbed her arm, almost dropping her books, and smiled eagerly. "How's it going?"

Betsy gave her a suspicious look. "Fine," she said. "What do you want? You already told me all about what a god Scott Forester is, if that's what this is about."

"Oh." Suddenly Stevie remembered spending a good five minutes that morning explaining to Betsy and several other classmates exactly why they should vote for Scott despite anything that Veronica might say. "Right. Well, I just wanted to remind you that Election Day is tomorrow."

"Duh." Betsy rolled her eyes and shifted her books to her other arm. "Anyway, I haven't even decided who to vote for yet. So you might as well save your breath."

Stevie didn't bother to point out the mixed-up logic of Betsy's statement. She could already guess the competing forces at work in Betsy's mind. She was a member of the clique of popular kids and wannabes that revolved around Veronica diAngelo, which meant that she paid an awful lot of attention to whatever Veronica thought. However, she was also completely boy-crazy—if anyone was likely to cast a vote because of a candidate's hunky good looks, it was Betsy.

"Okay," Stevie said, wishing she'd thought to have some flattering pictures of Scott printed up to pass out to people like Betsy. "Uh, I was just wondering if you noticed Scott at the dance the other night. Didn't he look nice in that jacket he was wearing?"

Betsy smirked. "Sure, Stevie. Whatever you say. He looked totally delicious."

"Yeah," Stevie agreed, encouraged by the comment, though she couldn't quite figure out the weird expression on Betsy's face. "Well, I just thought—"

She cut herself off as she spotted Callie coming down the hall toward her, accompanied by Moira Candell, one of Betsy's best friends. The two girls seemed to be discussing a history quiz, but they both paused when they reached Stevie and Betsy.

"Hi," Callie greeted Stevie with a smile.

Stevie smiled back, but she kept her gaze on Betsy and Moira, not wanting to be distracted from her campaigning by small talk.

"What's going on?" Moira asked, casually tucking her chin-length auburn hair behind one ear and looking curiously from Betsy to Stevie and back again.

Betsy grabbed her by the arm. "Check it out," she said with a grin. "Stevie was just reminding me how hot Scott Forester looked at the dance."

"Really?" Moira's green eyes narrowed and she looked at Stevie with interest.

"I guess you could say that," Stevie said. She didn't like Moira much—those catlike eyes of hers hid a mean streak as wide as the Potomac—but she was still a potential voter, and this seemed like a good chance to kill two birds with one stone. "Actually, I was just about to remind Betsy—back me up here, Callie—that Scott worked really hard to make that dance happen. He knew people would enjoy it, so he took action to make them happy."

Moira raised one carefully groomed eyebrow and shot Betsy a quick grin before turning back toward Stevie. "So what kind of action does he take to make *you* happy, Stevie?"

"What?" Stevie frowned, not understanding the comment.

Betsy giggled with delight. "Come on, Stevie," she said. "You can level with us. We know why you're campaigning so hard for Scott. Veronica told us you two are hot and heavy."

Stevie gasped, finally getting it. "What?" she sputtered. "Are you saying—"

She broke off, not even wanting to put it into words. It was too ridiculous. She glanced at Callie, expecting her to leap to her defense, tell the two girls that Stevie and Scott had no romantic interest in each other. But instead, Callie was staring at Stevie with a startled, thoughtful, questioning look on her face.

Stevie felt her heart jump. She couldn't believe that Callie might actually believe one of Veronica's smarmy lies.

"Listen," she told Moira and Betsy sharply. "I shouldn't even have to tell you this, but there's absolutely nothing going on between me and Scott. I'm his campaign manager and his friend—that's it. Anything else you've heard is just another one of Veronica's pathetic lies."

Moira shrugged. "Whatever. It's not like I care one way or the other." She gave Stevie a scornful glance before turning away. "Come on, Betsy. Let's hit the soda machine before second period."

The two girls wandered away. Stevie turned to Callie with a scowl. "Okay, what was that all about?" she demanded, her hands on her hips.

Callie looked startled. "What was what all about?"

"I saw the look you gave me," Stevie replied

bluntly. "When Betsy said that about me and Scott. You looked like you might actually believe it."

"I'm sorry," Callie said immediately, giving Stevie an apologetic smile. "I didn't mean to. I know that you and Scott are just friends, and that you would never even think about cheating on Phil. It's just that, well, for a second it kind of made sense that someone might think otherwise, you know, because of all the time you've been spending together. I guess it was sort of an automatic reaction, like a 'what if' thing. I'm really sorry if it looked like I didn't trust you, or like I actually believed Veronica's vicious gossip."

Stevie nodded, appeased. "That's okay," she said. "I guess I'm being a little touchy. I was just so surprised." She forced a laugh. "I mean, I've been hearing rumors about Scott and you and the rest of your family all weekend, but this is the first one that's involved me."

"I understand," Callie said. "It's always upsetting when—"

"Callie!" an overloud voice broke in. "There you are. I was hoping I'd catch you so that we could walk to chemistry together."

Frowning with irritation at the interruption, Stevie turned to see George Wheeler hurrying toward them. She felt a twinge of guilt as she realized she hadn't even asked Callie how her date with him had gone. Still, she supposed she could apologize for that later. At the moment, she was getting the nagging feeling that there was someone else who just might deserve an apology, or at least an explanation.

Maybe Phil wasn't so off base when he made that crack about Scott, she thought, hardly noticing as George put his hand on Callie's arm and steered her away, being careful not to get in the way of her crutches. *I mean, after all our years together, he definitely should know better than to think I could ever be interested in anyone but him. But maybe I haven't been totally fair, either.*

That wasn't an easy thing for her to admit, even inside her own head, but she forced herself to face it. Hearing the second-period bell ring, she automatically headed down the hall toward her math class.

I mean, if Callie could believe there was something going on between me and Scott, even for a second, I probably shouldn't be surprised if the thought has crossed Phil's mind, too, Stevie told herself ruefully. *And the way I've been spending all my time talking about the election probably hasn't helped much, either. It's no wonder if Phil is feeling a little neglected and insecure.*

She shook her head, suddenly feeling guilty about the way she'd been taking her boyfriend for granted. In fact, she realized, she'd hardly spent a moment thinking about him in the past couple of days, despite that upsetting phone call on Saturday night.

There's only one solution, she thought as she walked into her classroom and hurried toward her desk. *When I get home today, I'll have to beg Mom and Dad* to let me use the phone, no matter how many extra hours of chores I have to do in exchange. Then I'll call Phil and make sure I don't hang up again until I've totally convinced him that he's the one and only guy for me.

THIRTEEN

"Are you ready for this?" Stevie asked the next morning, feeling an anxious knot tightening in her stomach as she caught her first glimpse of the school building out the car window.

From his position in the driver's seat, Scott glanced at her in the rearview mirror and grinned. "Ready for what?"

"Very funny." Stevie rolled her eyes and drummed her fingers nervously on the leather back-seat of Scott's car. It was Election Day, and Scott had offered to pick her up so that they could face the big day as a team. Stevie had quickly accepted the invitation. She had wanted to get in early again, and she'd doubted she'd have been able to convince Alex to abridge his breakfast two days in a row.

Callie glanced at Stevie from the front passenger's seat. "He's always like this on the big day," she said. "Dad, too. Pretty annoying, huh?"

"Definitely." Stevie couldn't believe how calm Scott was acting. He'd been cracking jokes during the entire drive, and his hands were as steady as ever on the wheel. Stevie felt like such a wreck that she wasn't sure she would have been able to drive.

Before long they were pulling into the student parking lot. There were only half a dozen cars parked there so far—few students bothered to arrive a full half hour before the homeroom bell unless they had an early club meeting or music rehearsal. Stevie took a deep breath of the cool morning air as she climbed out of the car.

"Here goes nothing," she said as the three of them headed for the front steps.

"Ready to do a little last-minute campaigning?" Scott asked her.

Stevie nodded. The actual voting would take place during homeroom, so she knew they didn't have much time. But she planned to make the most of what little they had. "Let's go to it."

As soon as they got inside, she and Scott went to work, wandering the halls and talking to everyone they could find. Valerie Watkins and the other two candidates were there, too, doing the same thing. Stevie did her best to ignore them and concentrate on convincing as many people as she could that Scott was the best candidate.

The homeroom bell rang, startling her out of her description of Scott's plans for refurbishing the ancient locker rooms in the gym. The sophomore guys she'd been talking to wandered off, and Stevie took a deep breath, realizing she'd run out of time.

"Better hurry up, Stevie," a snide voice came from

behind her. Turning, Stevie saw Veronica diAngelo strolling toward her own homeroom. "You don't want to miss your chance to vote for your new boyfriend."

A thousand sharp retorts flew into Stevie's mind. But she ignored all of them. Instead, she smiled sweetly at Veronica. "May the best candidate win," she said calmly, turning away without bothering to watch Veronica's reaction.

As she walked into her own homeroom a moment later, Stevie was feeling calmer than she'd felt in a week. All of her former nervousness had fled. She and Scott had done what they could. It was up to the voters now.

Her homeroom teacher looked up as she entered. "You're late, Lake," he said. "Grab a ballot—you don't want to miss your chance to do your civic duty, do you?"

"Thanks, Mr. Knight," Stevie replied, accepting the sheet he held out to her. Hurrying to her seat, she pulled out a pen and let her backpack drop to the floor with a thud. Clicking the pen open, she flattened the one-page ballot sheet on her desk and drew a bold check mark in the box beside Scott's name.

Carole stared at the blank notebook page on the desk in front of her, but she didn't see it. Instead she saw a perfect vision of Samson flying over the obstacle course of four-foot fences she'd set up for him the previous afternoon. He'd had no more trouble with it than he would have had with a row of cavalletti lying on the ground, and Carole was bursting with the growing certainty that the big black horse could handle anything the Colesford course designers threw at them in Open Jumping. She only hoped she would be able to handle it, too—she didn't want to let Samson down. She could already imagine how wonderful it would feel to stand at his head as a judge clipped a fluttering blue ribbon to his bridle. . . .

Chewing absently on the end of her pencil, she let out a deep sigh of anticipation. Noticing that the girl across the aisle was shooting her curious looks, Carole snapped out of her daydreams and blinked, trying to focus her mind as well as her eyes on her biology notebook. She was supposed to be writing out the steps she planned to follow for the lab project the class was starting the next day—most of her classmates were scribbling away busily—but she just couldn't seem to concentrate on the task. Whenever she wasn't dreaming of her brilliant future with Samson, she was doing her best to get used to the idea that Starlight wouldn't be a part of that future. The idea of giving him up still hurt a lot, but she was starting to accept it, at least a little. She knew in her heart that it was for the best. She couldn't give him what he needed, and she loved him too much to let him go without.

Once again, she tried to concentrate on her

schoolwork. CELL REPRODUCTION PROJECT, she wrote at the top of the page. ACTION STEPS FOR LAB.

Then she paused, chewing on her pencil again. This time she found her thoughts wandering to Ben. She hadn't seen much of him the afternoon before because he'd been busy helping Red reorganize the toolshed. That meant she still hadn't found a chance to thank him for distracting Max on Sunday.

I'll have to make a point of saying something to him before I forget, she thought, doodling the letter *B* in the margin of her notebook. She added ears, a mane and tail, and four legs to the *B* so that it looked like a fat little horse sitting up on its tail end. Smiling at the silly drawing, she scribbled over it and then glanced around to make sure nobody was watching her.

Nobody was. The teacher was sitting at the front of the room correcting papers, and everyone else was concentrating on their own work.

Carole slumped down more comfortably in her chair and gazed at her notebook again. She knew she should be thinking about those lab action steps. But the only actions she felt interested in planning at the moment were her own for the next couple of weeks. She was going to be busy, and she wanted to be ready.

The horse show's a week from Saturday, she thought. *That gives me ten more days to get Samson into his peak condition. At the same time, of course, I need to work on finding the perfect new owner for Star-light.*

She paused to think about that second task for a moment, trying to hold down her emotional response to the idea of finding a buyer for her beloved horse and think about it logically. It helped a little to imagine how Lisa might look at it.

She would probably point out that matching up a perfect horse-and-rider pair is always tricky, Carole thought. *But then she'd also remind me that Starlight is such a wonderful horse that anyone would be lucky to have him. He's well trained, healthy, and sound. He's still young enough to offer years of performance and companionship. He doesn't have any serious vices. And he's more than talented enough to win somebody a whole roomful of ribbons, to match the ones he's won with me.*

That made her feel a little bit better, and it made her feel better still to know that Stevie was already on the job, helping her find that perfect owner. She wasn't sure she'd have been able to handle it by herself, especially with everything else that was going on.

If I'm lucky, she thought, *maybe we can even get it all taken care of before the show.* Realizing that that was pretty unlikely, she amended the thought. *Or at least get the process well under way. Maybe find a couple of likely prospects. Then, when Samson and I turn in a brilliant performance at the show*—she paused long enough to rap lightly on the wooden top of her desk for luck, bringing another inquisitive glance from her neighbor across the aisle—*and Dad is feeling proud of me, I can bring up the idea of maybe, possibly, somehow, figuring out a way to buy Samson from Max.*

That last part was the only thing that was making her a little nervous. Samson was a valuable horse, and Max really couldn't afford to let him go for less than he was worth. Still, Carole knew that she would find a way to meet the price somehow. The money from the sale of Starlight would help, of course—he was worth much more now than what her father had paid for him, thanks to all the training Carole had done over the years.

Again, Carole felt a pang when she thought about the reality of actually selling Starlight. But she was trying not to dwell on that. She needed to focus on the bright side of the situation, and that was Samson. She couldn't wait until he belonged to her, and she needed to do everything she could to make sure it happened as soon as possible.

Returning her thoughts to the topic of money, she scribbled a few numbers in the margin of her notebook, trying to figure out how much she would need. Luckily, her birthday was coming up the week after the horse show. *That has to be good for a few more bucks from Dad,* she thought. *Plus, I've got a little money saved up from work. . . .*

Finally she gave up on trying to estimate the financial details. Max was a reasonable guy, and he knew how well Carole and Samson went together. She was sure he would let her work out some sort of installment plan, if that was what it took. The whole idea of her owning Samson was so perfect, so right, that Carole was positive it would work out somehow.

Whatever I have to do, it will all be worth it, Carole thought. An image of Starlight flashed into her mind again, but she blinked it away and stared fixedly at her notebook. *It will definitely be worth it when Samson is all mine.*

". . . and so I figure if I don't think about all the show experience the other riders have, I won't be able to psych myself out, and I might actually have a shot to do really well."

Callie leaned her elbow on the lab table and did her best to seem as though she were listening to George. "Hmmm," she said when he paused for breath.

"All I need to do is prepare myself and my horse as best I can and then focus on our own performance instead of worrying about anyone else."

Callie sighed. George had turned up to walk her to chemistry class again that day, and again she hadn't known how to escape. Because they were lab partners, they sat together in class, and for the past five minutes, while the teacher explained something to another student, George had been sharing his views on the Zen of horse show preparation with her. She wasn't sure she could stand it much longer. She wasn't sure she could stand *him* much longer. No matter how many times she told herself that he was a nice person, that it wasn't his fault that he was nerdy and annoying, she couldn't seem to make herself like him any better.

"Anyway, no matter how I do, it's a real treat for me just to be—" Suddenly George broke off in mid-sentence. "Oh! I almost forgot." He leaned over to dig into his backpack, exposing a pale sliver of skin between his pants and the hem of his shirt. Callie averted her eyes and did her best simply to appreciate the moment of quiet. When George sat up again, he was clutching a foil-wrapped package about the size of a hardcover book. "I was going to give this to you this morning, but then Stevie interrupted us," he said, presenting the package to Callie.

"Um . . ." Callie wasn't sure what to say. She turned the package over, trying to figure out how to react. "What is it?"

"Open it." George grinned. "It's for you."

With a feeling of dread, Callie peeled back the shiny gold paper until she could see the label on the box underneath. "Chocolates," she said blankly.

"I remembered how much you said you love chocolate. You mentioned it at the dance." George looked proud of himself. "Do you like them?" He peered at her expectantly.

Fortunately, their teacher walked to the front of

the room at that moment and called for attention, so Callie was saved from answering.

Still, she knew she had to do something before the situation with George got any further out of hand. She had to end this relationship, if you could call it that, before she got so frustrated and annoyed with him that she wouldn't be able to talk to him politely anymore and would say something that would really hurt him. Clearly the problem wasn't going to go away on its own, as she had hoped.

"Listen," Callie said as the teacher turned to begin writing the lab procedure on the chalkboard. "I need to talk to you about something. Can you meet me in the south stairwell before lunch?"

George's face lit up. "Sure," he agreed quickly. "I'll be there as soon as I get out of fourth period."

Callie nodded, turning away to avoid the eager, trusting look in his eyes. Now all she had to do was spend the next three class periods figuring out what to say.

FOURTEEN

A s she changed into her gym clothes before phys
ed, Stevie struggled to hold on to her positive
feeling from earlier that day. But it wasn't easy.

"Anyway," Veronica diAngelo said loudly, "I'm
sure Valerie will make an excellent president. She has
so many good ideas. And unlike some people, her
ideas actually *are* her own."

Stevie gritted her teeth. Veronica was ostensibly
talking to her friend Nicole, but it was perfectly obvious that she was aiming her comments at Stevie
and Callie, who were only a few yards away. It was
only third period and the election results weren't in
yet, but Veronica seemed to be assuming that she'd
gotten what she'd wanted, as usual.

Callie shot Stevie a sympathetic look, seeming to
guess what she was thinking. "Hang in there," she
murmured, leaning against the row of lockers as she
watched Stevie pull on a pair of sweat socks. "It'll all
be over soon, one way or the other."

"I just wish Miss Fenton would hurry up and
announce who won already," Stevie grumbled, shov-

ing her feet into her sneakers. "Put us all out of our misery."

Veronica's voice got a little louder as she continued talking to Nicole. "Besides, it would be better if we had a president who couldn't be influenced by so-called campaign managers who are actually just overinvolved girlfriends."

Stevie closed her eyes for a second, but she didn't make a sound. Callie shot her a surprised look. "Are you okay?" she asked.

"I'm fine." Stevie smiled pleasantly. "Just fine." She leaned over to tie her shoes.

When she sat up, Callie was gazing at her in surprise. "Are you sure you're okay?" she asked hesitantly. "I mean, didn't you hear—"

"I heard her," Stevie interrupted. "And yes, I'd really like to walk over there and tell her off. But it's not worth it. It doesn't matter."

"Really?"

Stevie shook her head. "I realized something yesterday," she said. "People are always ready to believe the worst about other people. It's, like, human nature or something."

Callie blinked. "What do you mean?"

"It doesn't make people bad, necessarily," Stevie explained. She'd been thinking about this topic a lot over the past twenty-four hours. Scrubbing out her mother's sizable collection of empty clay flowerpots after her phone call to Phil had given her plenty of time to ponder it. "It's like the way you almost believed for a second that Scott and I could have been sneaking around together." She shrugged. "And it's the same way that Phil was starting to think, too, just because I've been talking about Scott so much lately."

"Wow." Callie looked surprised again. "I didn't know he felt that way."

"I didn't realize it myself until yesterday," Stevie admitted. "I mean, it's kind of ridiculous that the thought would even cross his mind. It doesn't really mean he doesn't trust me or anything like that, but actions speak louder than words, I guess. So that's why I called him up right after school to apologize and let him know he's still number one in my book, even if I haven't been acting like it lately. That was all it took to make Phil feel better, and it kind of made me feel better, too."

Veronica and Nicole walked past at that moment on their way out of the locker room. "Did I hear right?" Veronica said in mock surprise. "Did you just mention Phil? I assumed things were all over between you two, now that you and Scott are an item. Or aren't you planning to tell him about that?"

Stevie rolled her eyes. "Do us all a favor, Veronica," she snapped. "Go stick your finger in a light socket."

Veronica and Nicole just smirked and continued on their way. Callie shook her head and watched them go with a little frown on her face.

"Okay, Stevie," she said when the other girls were

out of earshot. "I think I see what you're saying. But if it's true, then doesn't that mean Scott is probably in trouble? I mean, look at it this way. He's the action candidate, and like you said, actions speak louder than words."

"Right." Stevie grabbed an elastic from the top shelf of her gym locker and gathered her dark blond hair into a ponytail. "So?"

"So you also said that people are willing to believe the worst—meaning, in this case, all Veronica's nasty lies and rumors. So if that's true, too, then all Scott's actions could still be for nothing because Veronica will be able to convince everyone that he didn't really do anything."

Stevie thought about that for a second. "I don't think so," she said at last. "Actually, I think the opposite is true. Veronica's lifetime of sneaky, dishonest actions will make people know better than to believe anything she says for long, even if they listen to it at first. So that's another way of actions speaking loudly. Or something like that." She grinned and threw up her hands. "I don't know. I think I'm starting to confuse myself now. Lisa's the logical one, not me." She swung her locker door shut and stood up. "All I know is that after all we've been through in this election, Scott *has* to win."

Callie smiled. "Is that your logical side talking?"

"No way." Stevie shook her head grimly. "Logic doesn't have anything to do with it. He has to win because I couldn't bear for things to turn out any other way."

George was already waiting when Callie arrived at the south stairwell just before lunch. She had chosen the spot purposely because she'd known it was likely to be deserted at that hour—the cafeteria was located across from the north stairwell, so almost everyone went that way to get to lunch. Sure enough, George was alone, leaning against the baluster at the bottom of the stairs.

"Hi." Callie stepped forward to meet him. Her voice echoed slightly in the deserted three-story stairwell. She glanced up briefly at the shafts of sunlight cutting through the stale, dusty air from the narrow vertical windows on the landings above. Then she turned her attention back to George. "Thanks for meeting me."

"No problem," George replied, taking a step toward her. "I'll meet you anytime, anywhere, Callie."

Callie cleared her throat, causing another echo. "Um, that's kind of what I wanted to talk to you about. I, um, I think maybe things are moving a little too fast here."

It wasn't exactly what she wanted to say. She wanted to tell him that she had absolutely no interest in going out with him ever again and she was absolutely positive that her feelings were never going to change. But she figured that was a little harsh—there was no need to be cruel about this.

George looked crestfallen. "What do you mean?"

"I just don't think things are working out," Callie said gently. "You know, between us."

"But they are," George protested. "I mean, we had fun at the dance the other night, right? And we have so much in common."

"I know." Callie didn't bother to correct his assumption that she'd had as good a time at the dance as he had. "It's not that. And it's not that I don't like you. It's just that I don't like you in *that* way, you know?"

"I see." George was silent for a moment. His round, pale face wore a slight frown, but otherwise there was no sign of the heartbroken disappointment Callie had expected. In fact, he seemed surprisingly calm.

She hesitated for a moment before speaking. "Um, are you all right?"

"I'm okay." George gave his head a brisk shake, like a horse shaking off a pesky fly. Then he looked at her earnestly. "None of this means that we can't still be friends, right?"

Callie felt slightly confused, as if she'd missed a beat somewhere. She had been sure that George would freak out when she broke things off with him. But he didn't even seem upset. It was a little strange. She couldn't have misjudged his feelings so completely, could she?

Realizing that he was waiting for an answer, she forced a smile. "Sure," she said. "Of course. I hope we'll always be friends."

"Good." George looked satisfied. "All right, then. I guess that's settled." He tilted his head to one side and smiled. "So is it all right if a friend walks another friend to lunch?"

"Um, sure." Callie still felt confused, not to mention a little guilty. But as they left the stairwell together and headed for the cafeteria, she mostly just felt relieved that it was all over.

By the time sixth period rolled around, Stevie's calm mood had evaporated completely. She was a nervous wreck as she walked into chemistry class and took her seat beside Scott.

"Hey," he greeted her. "Hanging in there?"

"Not really," she replied. Her anxiety had increased with every passing hour. She'd flubbed every answer when her teacher called on her in her fourth-period English lit class. And she'd spent most of her lunch period and her fifth-period study hall glancing at the PA speaker every two seconds. "What about you?"

He shrugged and smiled pensively. "Let's just say this isn't my favorite part."

Stevie nodded. She knew exactly what he meant. "I'm just glad you're the actual candidate instead of me," she told him. "Otherwise I really don't think I could survive all this suspense."

Scott patted her on the arm. "Hey, just remember," he told her. "Whatever happens, I appreciate everything you did. You're an awesome campaign manager."

"Thanks." Stevie managed a small smile.

She was pulling her lab notebook out of her backpack when the PA system crackled to life. She sat bolt upright, her heart pounding.

Most of the other students murmured with excitement as their headmistress's familiar, reedy voice greeted them through the speaker. "This is it," Scott murmured under his breath.

Stevie shot him a quick glance and then turned back toward the speaker over the door, as if by staring at it she could make Miss Fenton's words come faster. *This is it*, she repeated to herself, crossing her fingers on both hands.

"Students," Miss Fenton's voice announced. "I'm sure that you're all eager to hear the results of this morning's special election for student body president. I won't keep you in suspense much longer, but I want to take just a moment and say that it was a close and interesting race. All of our candidates had marvelous ideas about ways to improve our school, and they all deserve our thanks and respect for wanting to take the responsibility of serving us in this important office."

"Yeah, yeah," Stevie muttered, tapping the side of her foot nervously against the leg of her lab table.

She was sure she would explode if she had to wait one more minute for the result. "Get on with it."

Miss Fenton did. "Without further ado," she said, "I am very pleased to announce that our new student body president is . . ."

Stevie held her breath. Beside her, she felt Scott tense and lean forward with anticipation.

". . . Scott Forester!"

FIFTEEN

After school that day, Stevie still felt as if someone had pumped her full of helium and sent her skyward. She couldn't believe how good it felt to have all her hard work on the election pay off.

Life is good, she thought as she pulled into the driveway of Pine Hollow. She smiled as she realized that it seemed like an odd thing to think. After all, she was still grounded.

But everything else really was pretty wonderful. Scott had won the election. She and Phil were back on track and better than ever. Belle was in terrific shape for next weekend's horse show. . . .

As she parked beneath the shade of the gnarled old pine tree that grew beside the gravel parking area, Stevie spotted Carole leading a saddled pony out of the stable building. Immediately she felt a bit guilty about her cheerful thoughts. How could she be so upbeat when one of her best friends was going through such a difficult time?

Tossing her sunglasses on the seat beside her and grabbing the brown paper shopping bag she'd stowed on the floor in front of the passenger's seat, she climbed out of her car and walked over toward the stable building, squinting in the brilliant autumn sunlight. Carole saw her and waved.

Stevie waved back. "Do you have a minute?" she asked when she reached Carole and the pony. "I found out something interesting last night about . . . um, you know." She glanced around, unwilling to mention the topic out loud, even though nobody was within hearing distance other than the pony, which wasn't likely to blab.

"Sure," Carole said. She gestured toward the main schooling ring, where Max was talking to a little girl and her mother. "Let me just drop off Nickel over there and I'll be right with you. Meet me in the locker room?"

"Okay." Stevie wandered into the stable building, blinking to adjust her eyes to the relative dimness. She headed into the big, square student locker room, which was empty at the moment, and stowed the shopping bag in her cubbyhole. Then she perched on one of the long, narrow benches. While she waited for Carole, she mentally relived the past few hours. After Miss Fenton's announcement, her chemistry class had erupted into cheers. The teacher hadn't even tried to maintain order as students jumped out of their seats and hurried over to slap Scott on the back and congratulate him on his victory. Quite a few of them had also congratulated

Stevie, and the recognition of her role in the campaign had really felt good.

Who knows? Stevie thought contentedly, closing her eyes and once again feeling the rush of excitement that she'd experienced when she'd realized they had won. *Maybe I could get used to life on the campaign trail. I may look back on this afternoon someday as the starting point of my illustrious career as a political powerhouse.*

She smiled, letting the thought drift off—for now. There was plenty of time for her to think about what she might like to do someday. In the meantime, it was fun to dream.

"Hi," Carole said, walking in and peering curiously at Stevie. "What's with the weird look on your face?"

"Nothing," Stevie replied quickly. "Um, guess what? Scott won the election."

Carole's face lit up. "Really?" she said. "That's great! I forgot that was today."

Stevie grinned. Some things would never change—for instance, if it didn't have something to do with horses, Carole would be likely to forget it, whether it was Election Day or her own home phone number. "It is pretty great," Stevie agreed. "But listen. I wanted to tell you, I got a response to that e-mail I sent my cousin Angie the other night—you know, about Starlight."

Carole's expression grew slightly tense, but she nodded expectantly. "And?"

"Well, she's at college now, so she doesn't do much riding herself anymore," Stevie explained. "But she's still in touch with a lot of people who do ride, and she knows a girl who's dating a guy whose fourteen-year-old sister is looking for a horse. And this girl only lives, like, an hour's drive from here!"

"Really?" Carole's eyes widened. She sank down onto the bench beside Stevie. "What else did Angie tell you?"

"Not that much," Stevie admitted. "But I already wrote back to her and begged her to find out all the details about this girl and what she's looking for. In the meantime, I'll keep trying to find more people who—"

"Hi!" Lisa interrupted, walking into the room at that moment. "Fancy meeting you two here. What are you talking about?"

Stevie shot Carole a quick glance, realizing she wasn't sure whether Carole had let Lisa in on her decision yet. "Um, not much," she said casually.

Lisa had been looking forward to telling her friends about her college decision—Carole already knew, of course, but Lisa still wanted to make it official with a big announcement. She hadn't come to the stable the day before because of a dentist's appointment, and she'd wanted to save the news to share in person. When she got a good look at her friends' faces, though, she decided to put that off for a moment. They both looked decidedly strange.

"What's going on?" she demanded. "Why do you guys look so weird?"

Carole took a deep breath. "I have something I wanted to tell you," she said, her face serious. "It's about what we talked about over the weekend— about making a choice between Starlight and Samson."

With a sharp pang of guilt, Lisa realized that she'd gotten so caught up in her own life that she'd nearly forgotten about that conversation. True, it had occurred to her once or twice over the past two and a half days to wonder if Carole had come to terms with her feelings about the two horses in her life, but she'd never really doubted which way her heart would take her. Carole had always been completely devoted to Starlight, and nothing could change that.

"What did you want to tell me?" she asked tentatively.

Carole glanced down at the floor and then up again, meeting Lisa's eyes. "I've decided I'm going to sell Starlight."

Lisa gasped involuntarily, and everything else flew out of her mind. "You're kidding!" she blurted out.

"No," Carole replied softly. "I'm not."

"I'm sorry." Lisa shook her head, trying to clear it and make some sense. "That wasn't very tactful. But I—well, I'm pretty surprised."

"I don't blame you. I was pretty surprised myself," Carole admitted with a tiny smile.

Stevie raised a hand. "That makes three of us."

"Wow. I can't believe good old Starlight will be leaving us." Lisa rubbed her cheek absently, trying to understand what this meant. Her college news popped back into her mind, but she pushed it aside. It wasn't the right moment for that. She could tell her friends later, after she'd had a chance to absorb what Carole had just told her. "I mean, it's kind of ironic, you know?"

"How do you mean?" Stevie asked.

Lisa leaned against the door frame and stuck her hands in the pockets of her khakis. "I mean, just when I'm about to become the owner of the horse of my dreams, Carole's dream horse is going away."

Carole played with a strand of curly black hair that had escaped from her braid. "Dreams can change sometimes," she pointed out. "It's true that Starlight was my dream horse when I got him, and for a long time afterward." She shrugged. "But Samson is my dream horse now. So soon we'll both be riding the horses of our dreams." With a quick glance at Stevie, she added, "I mean, all three of us will."

"Hmmm." Lisa wasn't sure what to say. Starlight had been around for so long that it was almost impossible to believe he might be leaving Pine Hollow soon. He was as much a part of the place by now as Prancer or Topside or Barq or any of the other school horses.

As if reading her mind, Carole sighed. "It will be really hard to say good-bye to Starlight," she said softly. "I know that. But I also know that this is the right thing to do. It will be better for both of us to move on."

Stevie nodded thoughtfully. "And that's pretty amazing if you think about it."

All three of them were silent for a moment, thinking their own thoughts. Carole could tell that both of her friends were still having trouble getting used to her decision. That wasn't surprising—she was still having some trouble getting used to it herself, even though she'd been thinking about little else for the past few days. But she'd meant what she'd said. She really did think this was the right thing to do.

She glanced up just in time to see Ben appear in the locker room doorway. He blinked when he saw the three of them inside the room and made a motion as if to back away. But when he caught Carole's eye, he stopped as if realizing he'd been caught.

"Uh, hi," he muttered. "Carole, I—"

Carole found herself blushing slightly, though she wasn't sure why. Earlier in the afternoon, she had finally thanked Ben for what he'd done the other day. He had brushed off her gratitude, seeming embarrassed, but his dark eyes had looked a shade friendlier than usual as he'd made an excuse and hurried off. "Yes?" she said shyly, remembering that rare smile.

Ben took a step backward, shooting Stevie and Lisa a slightly suspicious glance. "Um, never mind. I'll see you later." The next second, he was gone.

Stevie turned toward Carole with a smirk on her face and one eyebrow raised almost to her hairline. "My, my," she commented. "He's awfully chatty today. For Ben, I mean."

Lisa nodded and grinned. "What do you think that was about?" she added.

Carole pretended not to notice their sly expressions. She wasn't sure what was going on with Ben these days, and she didn't feel like talking about it until she figured it out. After what had happened between the two of them at Stevie's party, she wasn't about to jump to any conclusions and risk messing up their friendship yet again.

Fortunately she was saved from responding by the arrival of Scott and Callie. "Hey, check it out," Scott said as he entered the locker room. "The gang's all here."

"Hey!" Lisa looked startled as she turned to look at Scott. "I forgot to ask. Did you win?"

Stevie grinned. She'd been waiting for this moment since sixth period. "Allow me to answer that, if you will," she told Lisa mischievously. Hopping up, she raced to her cubby and retrieved the brown paper shopping bag. She reached inside, glancing around to make sure that everyone was watching, and then pulled out a two-liter bottle of ginger ale.

Carole looked confused. "What's that for?"

Instead of answering, Stevie held the bottle in both hands and deliberately shook it as hard as she could. The soda fizzed wildly inside the plastic bottle.

"Uh-oh," Scott said.

Stevie's grin widened. "Hey, I know it's not exactly champagne," she joked. "But after what happened at that party . . ."

Everyone laughed. Stevie made a move to open the bottle, but Scott was too fast for her. Lunging forward, he grabbed it out of her hands. "Aha!" he crowed, reaching to twist open the cap as Callie, Carole, and Lisa scattered, giggling and screaming.

Before Stevie could react, Scott released the pent-up soda, spraying ginger ale and bubbles in all directions. Stevie shrieked and danced away as the cold liquid hit her in the face, but she was laughing at the same time.

Yes, she thought giddily, *life is really pretty good.*

ABOUT THE AUTHOR

BONNIE BRYANT is the author of more than a hundred books about horses, including the Pine Hollow series, The Saddle Club series, Saddle Club Super Editions, and the Pony Tails series. She has also written novels and movie novelizations under her married name, B. B. Hiller.

Ms. Bryant began writing The Saddle Club in 1986. Although she had done some riding before that, she intensified her studies then and found herself learning right along with her characters Stevie, Carole, and Lisa. She claims that they are all much better riders than she is.

Ms. Bryant was born and raised in New York City. She still lives there, in Greenwich Village, with her two sons.